FAT VAMPIRE 2

FAT VAMPIRE 2

Tastes Like Chicken

JOHNNY B. TRUANT

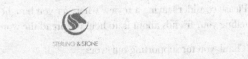

STERLING & STONE

For all the fat vampires out there.

ONE

Cold Prick

Reginald Baskin, who thought he might just be the fattest, slowest, and weakest vampire who ever lived, decided that he was going to need the emergency shirt he kept at the bottom of his desk drawer.

"So have you seen enough?" Reginald asked the customer between heaving breaths, the treadmill thundering under his feet.

The customer, an old man leaning on a bejeweled cane, nodded and said, "More or less. But can you give me another few minutes just to be sure? You don't mind, do you?"

"Not at all," Reginald lied.

Reginald was not built for treadmill running. His gut swayed side to side, all three hundred and fifty pounds of Body By Cinnabon shaking and rattling and punishing the machine beneath him. His breath came heavy and fast. He felt lightheaded. He raised an arm to wipe the sweat from his forehead, and received an unpleasant blast from his armpit.

Yes. He was going to need that shirt.

Reginald had been a vampire for six months, and there had been many times during those months that he'd wished Hollywood had gotten vampirism right. If Hollywood had gotten it right, Reginald would have had boundless strength, speed, and power from day one instead of passing out and breaking his nose the first time he'd tried to run. If Hollywood had gotten it right, he'd never have been tried by the Vampire Council as "an unfit embarrassment." If Hollywood had gotten it right, demonstrating one of his company's treadmills for a potential buyer would be a stupidly easy task, and he wouldn't feel like he was going to die.

Not that he *could* die right now, of course, even if he'd wanted to. And he kind of *did* want to. Where was a wooden stake when you needed one?

"It's just because I'm buying fifty of these machines, you understand," said the customer.

"No." *Breath.* "Prob." *Breath.* "Lem." *Wheeze.*

"And I'm incapacitated, or I'd do it myself," said the customer, nodding at his cane.

"Sure."

"And, frankly, I'm not…" He paused, looking down at his own slight frame. Then he raised his nose at Reginald's girth. "And *you* are…"

"Of course," said Reginald, cutting him off. The customer owned a Perfect Size Fitness franchise and would be buying the heavy-duty line of treadmills because they could take the most pounds of punishment. What he had almost said was that Reginald was fat enough to give the treadmills a realistic test. And while Reginald had made peace with the body he'd have forever, he didn't want to embarrass the customer by making him say it.

"What's the weight limit again?" said the customer.

"Five… Five hundred…" said Reginald, trying to catch his breath. Talking was becoming harder and harder.

"Five hundred pounds? I guess that's enough. And that's at maximum speed?"

"I guess… it's… *sure*," he said

Reginald wasn't a salesman and hence wasn't sure about the treadmill specs. The salesmen worked a different shift than Reginald. They all had perfect bodies and perfect faces and represented the company well, whereas Reginald was usually hidden away in accounting, further insulated by working the night shift. Why Phil Berger had called and insisted that Reginald accommodate this little old man now, in a ridiculous after-midnight meeting, was beyond him. Something to do with the old man's schedule, Berger had said.

"I imagine it could accommodate more weight at walking speeds than running speeds."

"I don't…"

"Because when you run, it's like slamming the thing with sledgehammers, I mean."

"I'm not…"

"Can you try it out at full speed?" said the man. And then *oh God oh shit oh damn*, the little old man was reaching toward the control panel and pushing the arrow that made the belt go faster.

"You don't mind, do you?" he said. "I just need to be sure."

"I'm." *Wheeze.* "I'm going to…"

Reginald's vision blurred. His feet came out from under him and he pitched face-first into the treadmill's console. The console cracked in half and Reginald fell to the belt, which rolled him off and into the corner behind the machine. His legs and rear wedged against the wall. His upper body, unable to roll further, remained on top of the deck. The running belt, still revolving because Reginald had pinched off the dead man's switch, was tugging his shirt down off of his shoulders and straining the buttons. Higher up, it was coating his face with friction burns.

With his last ounce of energy, Reginald rolled away from the belt and crumpled into the corner, breathing heavily. His heart was beating like a cross between a tympani and a telegraph. His shirt was soaked, sticking to him like tape.

That's when Maurice walked in.

Maurice looked at Reginald, at the treadmill, and then at the customer. His head made a small, odd jerk, and then he ran at the customer so fast that he seemed to vanish from the doorway and appear in front of the old man, who he punched in the face hard enough to throw him back into a treadmill that was folded against the opposite wall. The customer, struck above his center of gravity, rotated before impact and hit the folded treadmill face-first. The treadmill's deck broke in half and fell onto the man in a shower of metal bits and wires.

Reginald's mouth dropped open.

Then the broken treadmill's halves shifted and the customer got back up using his cane, which seemed to have flown across the room with him. He brushed at his hair with his free hand, dislodging shards of metal and plastic. His face was a mess of red pulp, his nose pointing inward, toward the back of his head. His wiry white hair stood up in a blood-soaked cowlick.

Maurice approached the stooped old man. Even Maurice, who looked like a nineteen-year-old goth kid, seemed imposing compared to the battered old man.

"I could kill you right here and right now," Maurice

told him. "And I think I might, for the disrespect you're showing the Deacon's office... *and* my Deputy."

"We were just having fun," said the old man.

The man made a neck-cracking motion, then stood up straight. The change in posture — and somehow in manner — made him look twenty years younger. Then his white, blood-matted hair became dark blonde and grew longer. His stooped frame elongated and filled out. Even his clothes changed, from a sober, tan suit to a black shirt with a scooped collar and a long black coat. The fancy cane retracted into his hand as if the hand were absorbing it. The hand became larger, as if swollen, and then the swelling dissipated up his arm and vanished.

"I'm sorry," said Reginald, standing and looking at the new man with the dark blonde hair. "I'm afraid I don't know what just happened."

"You lost the sale," said the man, brushing at his long black coat. The voice coming out of his mouth was that of Phil Berger. It was the voice that had commanded Reginald, over the phone, to meet with a mysterious new customer despite the late hour.

Maurice looked at Reginald. "Reginald, meet Altus," he said with disdain in his voice.

"Charmed," said Altus.

"Altus is an incubus. They're known for sneaking up on women in the middle of the night and having sex with them. One of their talents — not that they have many — is shape-shifting."

To demonstrate, Altus became Gary Coleman. He said, "What choo talkin' bout, Maurice?"

"Did you not notice how cold it was in here?" Maurice asked Reginald. "It's late May in Ohio. It doesn't get this cold in the dead of winter."

"I'm not seeing the connection," said Reginald, who was somewhat immune to cold and hadn't noticed.

When Maurice replied, it sounded like he was quoting something. "'You can identify an incubus by its unnaturally cold penis,'" he said. "You'd think that would be a useless bit of trivia unless you wanted to go around feeling crotches, but Wikipedia understates it a little. The things are like a brick of absolute zero. They suck all of the heat out of a room."

"Brick is right," said Gary Coleman, patting his groin.

"They're wastes. Pests. *Demons*, if you believe in that crap."

"It's not crap," said Gary Coleman.

"Rapists," Maurice continued.

"Hey!" said Altus, transforming back into the tall man with the dark blonde hair. "I haven't had to resort to rape in decades. These modern days, everyone wants to fuck a demon. The girls are all like, 'Your dick is so cold!' and I'm like, 'I'm an incubus, baby,' and they're like, 'Ooh, put it to me, bad boy!'"

Maurice gave Altus a look filled with loathing, but Altus seemed not to notice. He was busy fussing with his shoulder-length blonde hair. He stood several inches taller than Maurice and looked older, but that was unlikely seeing as Maurice was over two thousand years old.

"What do you want?" said Maurice.

"To pay my respects to the new vampire Deacon," he said. "And, of course, his dignified right-hand man, about whom we've all heard *so very much*." He made a rolling motion with his arm and bowed toward Reginald.

"I could pull your spine out through your mouth," said Maurice.

"But you won't," said Altus, straightening up, his expression suddenly serious. "Because even if I couldn't recycle and be right back here in a week, I know you and your curiosity. Right now, you're *dying* to hear why I came all the way down here, and what I must have to say."

"You've said it."

"Hardly. At the risk of being punched again, I could give a shit about paying my respects," said Altus. "The reason I'm here is because I know about the incident at the last Council meeting."

"Good for you."

"You don't want to know how I know?"

"Everyone knows," said Maurice.

And it was true; everyone did. At the May 15th Vampire Council meeting — which Maurice and Reginald had studiously and fortunately avoided — the roof of the main arena had inexplicably blown entirely off. It had come off in one giant piece, like the top coming off of a pickle jar. And that was bad, but what made it worse was that Council meetings were held during the day to permit sunlight executions. When the roof came off, the sun came in. Three hundred and sixty two vampires had been blown into dust, and the third that remained were found later that night, after the sun had set, hiding in the halls and buried under rubble.

"What if I said I know who was behind it?" said the incubus.

"It was a gas explosion," said Maurice.

"*Really*," said Altus.

"Really."

"You use a lot of gas at the Council?"

"I wouldn't know," said Maurice. "Something in the building the Council was using. Doesn't need to be *our* gas."

The incubus gave Maurice a knowing look. "What

happened two weeks ago was a warning. A ritualistic, by-the-book, prior-to-a-formal-warning… *warning*."

"Really."

"Yes. And at the next meeting — which you'll need to attend in person now that your proxy is dead — I'd bet you'll get the *second* warning. The formal one."

"This sounds very prophetic," said Maurice. There was a blur, and suddenly Maurice's hand was at the blonde man's throat. "Let's say that this *was* someone's fault and not some kind of an accident. Is it smart of you to come here with 'information' that sounds like a threat?"

Altus seemed unperturbed by Maurice's clawed hand on his neck. "You could see it as a threat," he said. "Or you could consider the possibility that maybe you don't know every damn thing, and that there are topics about which you are ignorant."

His head pinned by Maurice's hand, Altus's eyes swiveled to look into Maurice's eyes.

"Some groups — let's say *demons*, for instance — might have insight into certain areas about which vampires are largely ignorant — perhaps because the proud and mighty Vampire Nation doesn't usually pay much attention to things that it feels are…" Altus's eyes flicked to Reginald. "… *beneath it*."

Maurice slowly removed his hand from Altus's neck and stepped back.

"All right," said Maurice, rolling his eyes. "Lay some wisdom on us. What's the big insight we in our incredible arrogance are missing? What do you know? Who's out to… to *get* us?"

Altus pulled at the collar of his long black coat, straightening the area Maurice had wrinkled.

"Angels," he said.

TWO

Goth

"Angels," said Reginald, some time after Maurice had unceremoniously thrown Altus through a window. Altus had begun quizzing them about religious mythology. Then he'd turned into Alex Trebek and had started requiring Maurice and Reginald to give their responses in the form of questions. Then he'd suddenly found himself in the dumpster across the parking lot.

Reginald had said that Berger might notice the broken window.

Maurice replied that he'd glamour Berger into believing that a hawk had hit the window and had broken it. Then the hawk had apparently destroyed a treadmill. Damn vandalizing hawks.

Maurice lit a cigarette — his one remaining human habit, for which he refused to apologize — and rolled his eyes. "Fanatics," he said.

"So I take it you don't believe in angels?" said Reginald, opening a bag of pork rinds.

"Do you?"

9

"I didn't used to believe in vampires or incubuses. My standards have come down a lot this year."

"*Incubi*," corrected Maurice. Then he picked up a newspaper and began reading, the discussion apparently closed.

They were sitting in the break room. Reginald had changed into his emergency shirt. He was glad that Maurice, who had a high tolerance for the absurd, was the only other person around to see the shirt now that perfect-chin, perfect-teeth Todd Walker had gone for the night and Nikki was still in Paris visiting family. Reginald had thought that it was a plain black tee when he'd put it in the drawer, but it turned out to be a gag shirt he'd gotten for free with a toaster at a garage sale in downtown Columbus. It was black with white lettering and read, I THE JIGGY MOTHERFUCKER. It was huge, but was still at least a size too small on Reginald. The woman running the sale had said that Reginald could have it because it had been part of a set, and some other JIGGY MOTHER-FUCKER had already bought its twin.

Bizarre explanations aside, jiggyness aside, Reginald didn't understand why Maurice was so blasé about what had happened at Council.

After the catastrophe on May 15th, Reginald had reviewed the tapes from the Council camera system. What he saw was bizarre. The roof had simply *lifted* off. The arena was dark, and then suddenly there was a noise of rending concrete and steel and it became very bright. There hadn't been an explosion; the event had simply *occurred*. The idea that Maurice wasn't at least interested in hearing possible explanations was bizarre.

But then again, Maurice loathed the Council. What the Council called "catastrophe," Maurice called "awesome."

Five months earlier, Maurice had seized control of the Vampire Council by assassinating the prior Deacon in order to save his, Reginald's, and Nikki's lives. When the dust settled, Maurice was the new Deacon... but Maurice didn't *want* to be Deacon. The job was demanding. The entire Council loathed him. And what was worse, Deacons lived with the constant threat of assassination. So he'd asked Reginald to find him a way out of the burdens of Deaconship, and Reginald, who possessed the most vampirism-enhanced intelligence in recent history, had delivered.

After a bit of research, Reginald found an obscure legal provision that allowed the Deacon to nominate a by-proxy representative to take his place at meetings of the Council. The law was intended to allow a Deacon to govern if he was mortally injured or detained, but the law also had no time limit, so Maurice had by-proxied every meeting other than his very first as Deacon.

There was a side benefit as well: Succession-by-assassination only worked when the assassination occurred at a meeting of the Council, and because Maurice never attended, he could never be usurped by an assassin. If a Deacon died outside of Council, the Vice Deacon would take over. Vice Deacon was currently held by Gregor Wellings, who was schizophrenic.

So Maurice hung out at home and went to work, smoking his cigarettes and giving the finger to the council, freed from responsibility and more or less untouchable.

"We should really talk about what happened at the Council," said Reginald. "It wasn't angels, but it wasn't a gas explosion either."

"What it was, was awesome," said Maurice, not looking up.

"You're going to have to attend the next meeting. I still

haven't found you a new proxy that won't attempt a coup, now that Nicholas is dead."

"Pfft," said Maurice. "Let them coup. I don't care."

"Yes you do."

"No I don't."

Reginald grabbed the top edge of Maurice's newspaper, pushed it down, and made a serious face at his two-thousand-year-old maker.

"I don't mean to get all 'civic responsibilities' on you," he said, "but let's keep in mind that the Deacon alone has veto rights over new laws. Your presence or that of a trusted proxy are all that's keeping all kinds of stupid new crap from being passed."

"Oh, it's just politics as usual."

"No, it's not. Logan was a son of a bitch, but at least the Council and the Nation obeyed him. They've been reacting to *you* like an inflammation. Now that Logan is gone, the new proposals just keep getting dumber and dumber. It's like they're determined to prove that you're not the boss of them."

"Yet, I am."

"Only as long as you're present."

Maurice sighed and put down the paper. "Fine. I'll go. But I'm not happy about it."

The kitchen door swung open. What came in was dark and gloomy and of questionable gender. It seemed to be wearing a garment that could only be described as a cape with wizard symbols on it.

"Hey Frank," said Maurice.

"Hey," said Frank.

"You here for lunch?"

"Yeah," said Frank. He pulled up a chair and sat on it facing Reginald. He bent his neck to the side and raked away the cape's ties, then slapped his neck twice with two fingers.

Maurice looked at Reginald. "You're not feeding on Walker anymore?"

"Walker's getting anemic. I've fed on him every third day for a month. I swear last night I heard that gargling sound you get when you hit the bottom of a cup with your straw. The other day I saw him stumble into the copier in the hall twice."

"That's hilarious." Then he added, seriously, "Don't kill him, though. We can glamour Berger into believing a hawk destroyed a treadmill, but police investigations are a lot harder to squash."

"I don't want to kill Walker," Reginald assured him.

"Good."

"I just want him to suffer."

"Of course." Maurice turned to the newcomer. "How's your mom, Frank?"

"She's good. She bought that new minivan." And again Frank rapped his neck with his fingers, making the veins stand out.

In the past six months, Reginald had tried three times to hunt like a normal vampire, but his success rate hadn't improved even with a half year of practice under his belt. On one hunt, he'd been maced and then outrun. On another, he'd been kicked in the crotch. The third time he'd tried to hunt, he'd been shot in the face. After that, he'd decided that it would be Walker or willing prey from here on out. No more fighting losing battles.

"C'mon Reginald," said Frank, still tapping his neck and shaking his head to make his black hair jump off of his face. "Let's get it on."

"Jesus, Frank. Never say that. And turn around. It's

13

hard enough to put my mouth on you without you watching me."

"Just keeping it real, Mister B," said Frank. Then he got up and sat on the chair backward. Watching him revolve on the spot was like watching night turn to later that night on a doomed black planet.

Frank seemed to genuinely enjoy serving the vampire community. Reginald thought that volunteering to be fed on was kind of sick, but apparently sick was a popular thing to be. There had been no shortage of volunteers when Maurice had put a call out to his goth circles, and Reginald had turned away several applicants — including all of the girls, because feeding on your preferred gender was considered cheating in vampire couples.

Reginald bit into Frank's neck. Frank sighed in a way that was decidedly sexual.

"Bammit Fwank," said Reginald, his mouth muffled by the fat covering Frank's carotid artery.

"Pain is good, Mr. B," said Frank. Then the neck under Reginald's drinking mouth started moving as Frank began picking at the bag of pork rinds.

Two minutes later, Reginald pulled away, bit his own lip to draw a drop of blood, and smeared the blood on the punctures in Frank's neck to seal the wounds. Then he thumped Frank twice on the back like a member of a pit crew signaling a completed refuel.

"Thanks, Frank."

"No problem, Mr. B. You ready to turn me yet?"

"No, Frank."

"Any time. I can get chicks for us, you know."

Reginald doubted it.

"Thanks, Frank. Here." He started digging in his wallet.

"It's good, Mr. B," said the big goth.

"You sure?"

"You want to thank me, turn me."

"Can't do that. You know the rules."

"I guess so. Later Mr. B."

And with that, Frank was gone.

Maurice looked up. "You're an idiot," he said.

"Thanks."

"Feed on Nikki. She wants you to. Do it while you can, because her blood is going to be a lot better now, while she's still human. And you can't imagine what it's like to feed on someone you're bonded to. It's amazing."

"I can't." And he couldn't. He was still too human, and there was a taboo in human culture about biting those you were dating. Besides, it was a sexual act between couples, and even with six months between them, Reginald and Nikki still hadn't crossed that particular bridge. Reginald wasn't ready. Nikki was too good for him, he thought, and he had decades of rejection to unlearn.

"You're a vampire, you know," said Maurice.

Reginald made a *What do you want from me?* face and gestured at the door. "I just drank a kid's blood!" he said.

"Not good enough."

"I don't want to talk about it," said Reginald. Then he got up, grabbed his pork rinds, and left.

THREE

Balanced

Maurice was a good resource and a good friend, but he hadn't been much help to Reginald as a mentor on the physical aspects of being undead. It wasn't Maurice's fault. Reginald couldn't run like a vampire, so Maurice didn't need to show him how to corner without falling and how to move without knocking things over. Reginald couldn't lift big objects like cars, so Maurice didn't need to show him how to manage heavy loads. Reginald couldn't jump high, so Maurice didn't need to show him how to land softly. Maurice suggested that Reginald hire a human physical trainer, but Reginald said that sounded a lot of work with no discernible benefit.

So Maurice made a strange suggestion. He told Reginald to take a gymnastics class.

Reginald asked why, already shaking his head *No*.

"Because," Maurice explained, "when you don't have much, you need to learn to make the most of what you have."

Besides, Reginald had exhibited amazing mental gifts as a vampire. He could pick up languages almost instantly.

He could calculate huge numbers in his head. He had photographic recall of everything he'd ever experienced, both as a human and as a vampire.

"Those are nervous system functions," he said. "You know what else are nervous system functions? Things like balance. Coordination. Neural efficiency."

"I'm six feet tall and weigh three hundred and fifty pounds, and you want me to be a gymnast," said Reginald. "Perhaps you don't understand physics."

"I don't expect you to be a gymnast. I expect you to teach your nerves how to get the most out of the abilities you have. Did you read *Dune*? It's like what those witch ladies did in *Dune*. They weren't strong, but they could do amazing things because they'd trained their nervous systems to control every single muscle, including the ones most people don't have voluntary control over. They weren't supernatural; they'd just trained normal bodies to do things that most people could never do."

"I understand the concept. But I am not the Kwisatz Haderach."

"The what?" said Maurice.

"Never mind."

Reginald had mulled the idea for two weeks. Maurice kept bugging him, but Reginald was sublimely unmotivated to do anything physical. It was Claire that finally got him to do it.

"Come on, Reginald," she told him over the phone. "I'll bet you'd be really good at it."

Reginald, who'd never been good at *anything* physical, said nothing. He let silence hang on the phone until Claire got impatient and yelled at him to stop being so self-loathing. That was the phrase she used.

"I'm not self-loathing," he said. "It's just that sometimes, in some ways, I kind of hate myself."

"I even know a place. I take lessons there."

"You do gymnastics?" said Reginald.

He'd had no idea. But really, how much could a vampire know about a 10-year-old girl who he'd once stalked as prey? The fact that they talked on the phone wasn't even weird anymore, because nothing about the relationship that "Uncle Reginald" shared with Claire made any sense. At least it was better than Reginald spending his 2am lunch hour in her living room, watching *Columbo* reruns while her mother was drunk upstairs. He'd put an end to that. Once Reginald, Nikki, and Maurice had saved her from the Vampire Council and gotten her a blanket order of protection and it had become apparent that Claire was in their lives for the long haul, Reginald had declared that enough was enough and insisted that she get some sleep.

Claire gave him the phone number of a rec center and urged him to call, promising that it'd be good for him. It felt strange taking life advice from a 10-year-old.

So he'd called the rec center and inquired about adult gymnastics. The woman he spoke to told him that there *was* no adult gymnastics program. Reginald was about to thank her and hang up, but then he remembered how persistent Claire could be. He had to at least try or she'd never leave him alone.

"How about individual lessons?" he asked.

The woman had asked him to hold while she rang an extension. Eventually, a chipper, young female voice answered, and Reginald repeated his question.

"I can do lessons," said the girl. "I'm only there Thursdays, though. Does 9pm work for you?"

"Sure," Reginald said. He sighed.

"Were you a college gymnast?"

"No."

"Just interested in learning?"

"Apparently."

"Do you have a gymnast's build?" she said. "Just wondering how to set our sights for what you'll work on."

"I'm six-foot, three-fifty," said Reginald.

A dog barked outside Reginald's window.

"Are you still there?" said Reginald.

"Oh, yes," she said.

"You said Thursday at nine?"

"Um…" But she'd already committed.

"See you then," he said.

When he arrived at the rec center, wearing a huge grey sweatshirt and huge grey sweatpants, the instructor looked him over from top to bottom, made a "Hmm" noise, and then introduced herself as Rebecca. She was maybe five-two and was waifish enough that Reginald had originally thought she was a teen boy. She explained that they'd be joined by another student for a joint lesson.

"I'm just here Thursdays, and she's been training with me for a while, so I figured I'd lump you together, and…." Then she looked past Reginald, waved, and said, "Oh, hi!"

Dammit.

Reginald turned and found himself looking down at Claire, who was fighting unsuccessfully to hold back a smile. A tall woman was holding her hand.

I even know a place. I take lessons there.

The center wasn't dedicated to gymnastics use. Had Claire known that the only instructor was only available at one time, no matter how many students chose to join her? He thought she did.

And so, all of a sudden, Reginald found himself taking not an *adult* gymnastics class, but just a *gymnastics* class… with a little girl. This had to look bad.

Rebecca introduced Reginald to Claire and Claire to Reginald.

"Charmed," said Reginald, shaking Claire's hand.

"I've never met you before now," said Claire.

Then Reginald extended a hand to the tall woman beside Claire. "I'm Reginald," he said. Then, because he felt he should say something more, he added, "I'm not a creep."

The woman took his hand and shook it. "Victoria."

Reginald had never laid eyes on Claire's mother before. She didn't seem drunk or messy or even negligent. He found it hard to believe that he'd spent untold numbers of hours less than fifty feet from this woman while she slept off a bender.

"I have a nervous system disorder that affects my balance and am here on doctors' orders, and it was Rebecca's idea that she teach us both at once, and also, I thought I was taking individual lessons."

"Rebecca told us you'd be joining us," said Victoria, deftly ignoring his backstory.

"I'm not creepy," Reginald repeated.

"I'm sure," said Victoria.

"I'm also not a great gymnast," said Reginald.

Victoria smiled.

After a few minutes of stretching, Reginald asked if they could start with some balance activities, so Rebecca ignored him and lined them up for vaulting. Reginald protested. Rebecca said, "It's just like jumping a fence" in a way that was supposed to sound dismissive, but that to Reginald rang more like a threat.

They lined up in front of a thing that looked liked a giant flat mushroom with a springboard at its base, and while Rebecca adjusted the apparatus, Reginald whispered with Claire.

"She seems nice, your mother."

"She got laid off from one of her jobs," said Claire. "So to save money, to keep off of food stamps, she quit drinking. Interestingly, it worked out to be a wash. Apparently her second job made just enough money for a lot of booze."

"So I wouldn't be able to come over at 2am anymore anyway," said Reginald.

"Not unless you wanted to get shot," said Claire. "Once she got more conscious at night, it suddenly dawned on her how unsafe our neighborhood is. So she bought a gun. Could you get shot and live, Reginald?"

"Yes," he said. "I got shot a few weeks ago. I don't recommend it."

"When you heal from being shot, does your body spit out the bullet?"

"Sometimes," he said.

"Sometimes it just stays in there?"

"Yeah. It's okay. It doesn't hurt. And if it does, there are vampire surgeons. They can work fast enough to get stuff out before you heal over it."

"That sounds awesome."

"They're crooks with fast hands. It's closer to a smash-and-grab burglary than a medical procedure," said Reginald. Reginald didn't have a high opinion of vampire doctors. He'd gone in once for liposuction, reasoning that if he could put foreign items inside of his body (bullet slugs, his stunt at the Council trial), there was no reason he shouldn't be able to pull items out of his body. The doctor smirked knowingly and put him on an unsanitary table and, after numbing him up, began shoving a large tube into his abdomen. Reginald had watched as a suction tank beside him filled with white fat and red blood, then watched as his stomach re-grew in front of his eyes and the fat in the tank turned to ash.

"Claire," said Rebecca from the vault table, patting its top. "Your turn."

Claire sprinted toward the vault table, struck the spring board at its foot, planted her hands, and flipped once to land in the foam pit more or less on her feet.

Victoria had sat down in a folding metal chair and was watching. She clapped.

"Reginald, you just kind of swing your weight around the side. Don't try to do what she did. Just kind of sidle around it."

Reginald looked at Victoria, then back at Rebecca.

"You're kidding."

"It's simple. Just like hopping a fence."

He looked at Victoria. He wished she weren't watching this.

"I've never hopped a fence. I don't know what that looks like."

Rebecca nodded to Claire. "Claire, show Mr. Baskin how you'd hop a fence."

Claire showed him. Reginald's eyes darted quickly to Claire's mother, wondering if all of this looked as odd to her as Reginald thought it must. He felt a strong desire to remind Victoria that it hadn't been his idea to be part of a kids' gymnastics class.

"Now you do it."

Reginald ran at the vault table. At the end, he took a little hop as Claire had and came down on the springboard, which uttered a loud bark and collapsed. Reginald's momentum threw him into the table.

Rebecca walked up and looked at the springboard. It wasn't broken, but the springs inside had all turned sideways. Her face was perplexed, trying to assimilate the possibility that her two students might weigh different amounts.

"Hang on," said Rebecca. She righted the springs inside of the collapsed board, declared it to be "Claire's board," and then took a second springboard and shoved six heavy-duty springs between its leaves. This would be Reginald's board.

"Go ahead," said Rebecca.

"I don't think I'm a vaulter. Gravity hates me."

"Just give it a shot," said Rebecca.

Reginald tried again. The board didn't collapse this time, but it didn't spring him upward either. When Reginald landed on it, it simply flattened as if he were standing on a doormat. Reginald's body, committed to the fence-jumping vault, planted its hands and swung its legs out, but the whole of him was a foot too low and so he simply ended up wrapped the leg of the table, below the vaulting surface.

"I don't think you're a vaulter," said Rebecca.

"Clearly."

"If you come back again, I'll bring the nuclear option. It's a super springboard."

"Ah."

"You're a bit larger than most gymnasts," said Rebecca.

"Really?"

"It's okay. Little gymnasts are a dime a dozen. When bigger ones can pull things off, it's impressive."

"That's very optimistic."

Rebecca, who didn't see Reginald's sarcasm, smiled brightly.

As the lesson progressed, Rebecca ran them through a handful of other skills. They tried cartwheels, handstands, various contortions, and even a dangerous flirtation with a set of high bars, which Reginald nearly snapped in two.

Eventually, after failing through most of the gym's equipment, Rebecca moved them to a balance beam that had been mounted on the ground. Rebecca explained that the floor beam was there to allow students to practice balance beam skills without the risk of a large fall.

"Reginald," said Rebecca. "Walk down this way."

Reginald started to walk toward her.

"On the beam, obviously."

"Oh." Reginald walked back to the start of the beam and then walked toward Rebecca. Then he remembered that he was supposed to be on the beam and slapped his forehead.

"Hey, that was good," she said.

"What was good?" said Reginald.

"You didn't even slow down."

"Well," said Reginald with *faux* pride, "I *have* been walking for most of my life."

Rebecca pointed down at the balance beam, which Reginald realized he was standing on.

"Try it again. Walk down to the end, then turn and come back."

Now that Reginald was aware he was on the beam, it was harder. He took a step, faltered under his weight, and put his foot on the floor beside the beam.

"Hang on," he said.

When Reginald had discovered each of his mental abilities, the process of letting his deeper, vampire mind take over had felt like entering a fugue. He didn't understand the process. He simply had to surrender and trust whatever was within him to take the reins. It was that way when he recalled long-dormant facts. They simply arose, and he didn't know the truth until he heard himself voice them. Maybe learning balance was like that.

So he closed his eyes, took a deep breath, and began walking as he just had, not looking down, not putting his arms out, trusting his feet to find the beam.

He opened his eyes and looked down. He was still on the beam, so when he reached the other end, he turned on one foot and walked back.

"I wouldn't have thought you'd be able to do that as easily as you just did," said Rebecca. "Don't take this the wrong way, but the physics aren't right."

Reginald thought back to what Maurice had said, about all of those little muscles being there already, and about how he'd just need to get them working together. *It doesn't take a lot of muscle to balance*, he'd said. *It just takes the neural ability to coordinate those muscles. And neural ability is one thing you definitely have.*

"Try it backward," said Rebecca.

So Reginald walked the beam backward. The trick seemed to be to focus only on the largest level of the goal and not the specifics: *Get to the other end*, not *put one foot in front of the other and hold your balance.* Something deep took over and seemed to know what to do when he left the details out of the equation.

"Skip," said Rebecca.

"I don't know how to skip."

"Like this," said Claire, who then showed him on the gym mat.

So Reginald skipped down the beam, very conscious of Victoria watching him.

After that — and probably because she'd finally found something Reginald could do — Rebecca seemed determined to give Reginald more and more difficult balance tasks until he failed at one. She had him jump, spin, and traverse it in giant, gazelle-like leaps. Finally, becoming bored, Reginald hopped off the beam and walked to the opposite side of the gym.

"Let's just go for the big finish," he said, picking up a basketball that had been left in the corner.

Reginald placed the ball on one end of the beam. Then he stood on the basketball and, like a stunt bear in a circus, rolled it under his feet across the beam to the other end.

Rebecca's mouth was hanging open.

"Watch this," said Reginald. He gripped the ball with his feet and hopped with it onto the floor. Then, the ball compressing underneath him, he rebounded back up onto the beam. He traversed half of the beam that way, bouncing on and off with the ball under his feet, until the ball exploded and Reginald fell across the beam, breaking his shin. He quickly turned away from the three humans, torqued it, and felt the bone knit back into place.

Rebecca said, "Try it on your hands."

"I can't support my weight on my hands," said Reginald.

"Try."

So he tried, attempting a handstand against the wall. And fell untidily into a heap.

"Next time," said Rebecca, slapping him on the back. "Good job today."

Reginald bade goodbye to Rebecca, Claire, and Victoria, and promised to at least consider returning for a second lesson the following week. Then he showered, changed, and headed to work. Maurice asked for a status update as soon as he saw him arrive.

"Balance beam good, everything else bad," Reginald reported.

Maurice asked for details, and Reginald gave them. He

told Maurice about the beam, the ball, and the showing off. Maurice seemed pleased.

"Did you try it on your hands?" he asked.

"I can't do a handstand," said Reginald.

"I'll bet you can," said Maurice. "I've seen you do pushups. I'll bet you could do a handstand."

"I tried. I can't do it."

"Try again," said Maurice.

"Maybe I could stand on my hands if we switched torsos," said Reginald, indicating Maurice's small frame. "A pushup is a long way from a handstand. Takes a lot of strength to hold this bad boy up." He patted his gut.

"I'm not telling you to do handstand pushups," said Maurice. "I'm just saying to hold yourself up. Most humans can physically hold themselves upright for a few seconds if they're braced right, and you're a vampire. Muscles tend to grow enough to service the body. Like, your legs. You may not think they're strong, but if it were possible for you to lose two hundred pounds, you'd find yourself in possession of some impressive pillars because they've been doing lunges all day long for years with three hundred and fifty pounds on them."

"I don't walk around on my arms," said Reginald.

"Ten bucks says you're wrong. Try it."

But they couldn't try it, because Reginald didn't know how to get into a handstand and neither did Maurice. So they looked it up and found a few videos online showing people bending over and putting their hands on the floor in front of a wall and then kicking their legs up overhead. Reginald couldn't touch his toes, and when he crouched to place his hands on the floor, he didn't have the leg or back strength to kick his torso and back up against the wall. Finally Maurice simply stood on a reinforced wooden box, picked Reginald up by both legs, and held him upside down above the ground. Reginald extended his hands over his head and placed them on the carpet.

"Ready for me to let go?" said Maurice.

"No."

"Ready now?"

"No."

"Now?" said Maurice.

"I love that you think the answer is going to change," said Reginald.

"Okay, letting go… now."

Reginald collapsed onto his face. His body became a giant floppy rag and fell into an untidy pile.

"Well," said Reginald. "That went well."

"You're too loose. Tighten up in your core."

"Where's my core?"

"In the middle of all of the fat."

So they tried again, with the same result. This time, rather than collapsing into a blob, Reginald's straight body fell like a tree, knocking down a cubicle divider.

Reginald, slightly out of breath, extended a hand toward Maurice. "Ten bucks."

"No. We didn't specify a timeframe."

"You dick. You turn me into a fat vampire and then you welch on a bet?

"Keep practicing," said Maurice. "All those little muscles just need to learn to talk to one another and obey that big brain of yours. Trust me."

Maurice hadn't been wrong yet and the ten dollars was going into escrow either way, so Reginald nodded reluctantly. He agreed to do both.

FOUR

Nosferatu

At midnight on June 1st, Maurice's cell phone rang and a computerized voice told him that the pickup window for his transportation to the Vampire Council would occur between 2:15 and 2:45am under an overpass on the outside of Columbus, near Hilliard.

Maurice sighed and put his face in his palm. "I don't want to go," he said.

"You have to go," Reginald told him. "You don't have a proxy. If you don't go, Gregor will be acting Deacon. Not only does Gregor usually think that there are small UFOs flying around his head, but when he's coherent, he's very liberal. And who knows what's on the docket that will pass if you're not there to veto it?"

"Ugh. And that long, long ride with blindfolds on..."

Reginald nodded, his lips pursed. This would be his third trip to the Vampire Council. The first time he'd gone, it had been for his own trial, and he'd been treated like a prisoner. The second time, he'd been free and he'd gone willingly, and he'd been treated like a prisoner. This time he and Maurice would be visiting as Deacon and Deputy of the Council, so *this* time, they'd be treated like prisoners. The procedure was the same for everyone, with no exceptions. They'd be bound with silver handcuffs and blindfolded twice, and then they'd be driven around for hours and handed off three or four times to different sets of escorts. The entire process was dictated by the master algorithm that choreographed all incomings and outgoings to and from the Council's current secret location. The system was what it was, and until the day Reginald divulged the fact that he'd cracked the algorithm, it's how the system would have to remain.

"Do you suppose we could just show up instead of meeting the escorts?" said Reginald. "Seems silly to spend all night traveling all over the place when I know the Council is currently in that half-finished theater we drive by all the time, like ten minutes away."

"If only," said Maurice.

"In fact, let's go there now," said Reginald. "We can hang out with Charles, who never leaves and travels with the Council every time it moves. Get some donuts."

"They don't have donuts at the Council," said Maurice.

"I know that. I said *get* some donuts. They have whole 24-hour stores filled with donuts now. We can give some to Charles as a peace offering. Not the good ones, though. Just those shitty plain ones with the little handles baked into them."

Maurice laughed.

Charles Barkley, who inexplicably refused to go by "Chuck" or "Charlie," had been a major force behind Reginald's accusation and trial. Following the trial, he'd wormed his way into a spot on the Council — a process over which the Deacon had no control. Once in, Charles had immediately begun pushing ultra-liberal legislation whose sole intention seemed to be to infuriate Maurice and insult Reginald.

"I *really, really* don't want to go," Maurice repeated.

"Get up," said Reginald. "It's time to make-slash-get the donuts."

And so, over a flurry of protests, Reginald loaded Maurice into his car and they drove to the pickup location at the scheduled time. Then, once cuffed and blindfolded, they spent several hours in the back of windowless SUVs pretending they didn't know where they were.

"I know we're *not* on Neil," said Reginald. "And I know we didn't juuust... *now* pass that Starbucks I go to all the time."

"Should I knock on the cab and ask them to stop, so that you can get a caramel latte?" said Maurice.

Thanks to the blindfold, Maurice was just a voice in the darkness, but Reginald's brain and senses had become refined enough that he could "see" his surroundings by listening to the way sounds bounced off of the objects around him. He clicked his tongue a few times and listened to the echoes to be sure he saw what he thought he saw.

"Don't make that face at me," he said to Maurice. "Just because *you* don't like coffee doesn't mean other vampires can't appreciate it."

Maurice said nothing.

Several hours later, Maurice and Reginald found themselves walking down a long and familiar-sounding hallway. Ten minutes after that, their handcuffs and blindfolds were removed and they made their way to the Council chamber, where they found Brian Nickerson sitting in a chair, texting on his cell phone. Brian was six-foot-seven and weighed over three hundred pounds of solid muscle. Under his bulk, the chair he was sitting on looked like a toy.

"Brian," said Maurice, "let that poor chair go."

"Maurice," Brian replied, standing and gesturing at Maurice's black wardrobe, "let Hot Topic go out of business."

Brian's massive frame was topped with a head of wiry, thinning brown hair. He had a square face and wore invisible-rim round glasses. Brian was the only vampire Reginald had seen who wore glasses. He didn't need them, of course, but they were a human affect that he rather enjoyed, like Maurice with his sword.

Brian had been 44 human years old when he'd been turned five years ago. By modern standards, 44 was quite old. With bootcamp becoming more and more stringent, it was rare for humans over 35 to make it through. Most graduates were under 30, and Charles kept trying to pass legislation that would place a formal age limit on applicants, regardless of their bootcamp performance — bad news for Brian's wife Talia, who at 37 hoped to wait eight more years to become a vampire, which was when she figured their youngest child would be old enough to be without her during the daytime.

Despite his young age as a vampire, Brian was one of the most senior Council members. Of the seven who had survived the last meeting, only one other had served under Logan. The rest had been killed by either Nikki or Maurice during the coup, and Brian had survived because Maurice had told Nikki to "avoid killing the guy who looks big enough to be three guys." The vote for Reginald's execution six months earlier had been eleven to one. Brian had been the sole holdout.

"You'd better watch your back, my friend," Brian told Maurice. "These others here, they're out for blood."

"Arguably, with a vampire population, that doesn't mean much," said Reginald. He looked up at Brian, who looked like a wall. Even at just five vampire years old,

Brian's enhanced strength would likely allow him to lift the Council arena. It was frightening to imagine him in a thousand years.

"Your blood too, Reginald," Brian said.

"They're always out for my blood," said Reginald, waving a dismissive hand. "I'm kind of used to it by now. I didn't fit in with my co-workers and I don't fit in with vampires. I didn't fit in through high school and college. I'm considering joining a fat running group because my sub-par speed would impress them. Maybe I could become their leader."

"The only thing stopping them from trying to kill you again is this guy right here," said Brian, laying his hand on Maurice's shoulder. Maurice's head came to Brian's nipples. If Brian had been hollow, it would take at least four Maurices to fill him if they were packed like Tetris blocks. "And you know the law. Right now, the law is protecting you, and the Deacon controls the law. But as soon as they find a way to change the law so that the Deacon no longer controls the law? Well, then, watch out."

"But Maurice controls the law," said Reginald.

"Until they change the law," said Brian.

"If they try to change the law, Maurice will block it," said Reginald. "Because he controls the law."

"Until he doesn't," said Brian.

It was futile to argue with Brian because he'd been a lawyer prior to being turned. There were many jokes about how Brian, who was too old to pass bootcamp, could only have gotten through because he'd been able to show years of prior experience as a bloodsucker.

"Brian," said Maurice. "You were at the last meeting, right? So what happened?"

Brian shrugged. "Gas explosion?"

"I mean, what did you *see?*"

Brian shook his head as if exasperated by a question he'd been asked a thousand times. "I don't know, man. Loud noises. Bright lights. Lots of ash and smoke. I even got a few seconds of sun myself, but I'm young, so it just singed me a bit. Then I grabbed Councilman Klein and used him as a shield. You remember Klein? Liked to eat babies."

"I remember Klein."

"Once he started to poof, the debris had mostly fallen and I dove the fuck under it. Bunkered in. Then a few hours later, the cavalry arrived. End of story."

"But what caused it? Was there... I don't know... an attack? Anything you saw that indicated foul play?"

"I don't see how. No blurs that looked like running vampires. The roof just kind of blew off."

Reginald stared at Brian. It seemed impossible that he could be hearing himself. *The roof just kind of blew off?* Were all vampires so jaded about death that they'd lost their fear of it? Were they so used to being the apex predators that they couldn't imagine anyone — or anything — being out to get them? Reginald had been right to assume the Guards' complacency back when they'd brought Nikki in. In death, vampires seemed to have lost the ability to see past the obvious.

"An incubus named Altus came to visit us about it," said Reginald. "And *he* says..."

"Altus!" Brian blurted, interrupting him. "I love that guy. He's an asshole. And yet, he knows he's an asshole. It's what makes him so awesome."

"*He* says there was foul play," Reginald finished.

"How could he possibly know?" said Brian. "It wasn't incubi, I can tell you that. They're not fast like we are."

"He says he just knows, and that it wasn't an accident."

"Interesting. So what kind of foul play removes a roof?"

"What kind of gas explosion doesn't make a huge noise and a fire?" Reginald countered. Reginald liked Brian, but Brian was being dense.

"There may have been noise and fire," said Brian. "It was pretty confusing. You lose track of things."

"Nothing is on the videos," said Reginald, who never, ever lost track of anything anymore.

"Really! Strange. Well, it's not like our guys do forensics. We got out of the wreckage, they glamoured those that needed glamouring, and the humans wrapped it up. Maybe we'll never know."

Now Reginald was just getting annoyed. "Why are you so blasé about this? Almost four hundred vampires died with no warning. Doesn't that bother you? You were in a building when the roof came off and death rained from above. You lay buried under rubble for hours."

"I don't know what to tell you, Reginald. Shit happens. A few years of knowing you can't *die* and can only *be killed* changes your perception. And no, I'm sorry, but I didn't see any vampires being foul, or playing, or getting up to any foul play. Besides, it was sunny out. They'd never survive to pull it off."

"Well, what if it wasn't vampires?" said Reginald.

"What would it be if it wasn't vampires? Don't tell me you think humans could pull a roof off. We have patrols in bunkers around the place at all times. Humans would need a crane, and nobody saw a crane, or any other kind of equipment."

Maurice put his hand on Reginald's chest. "Don't say it."

"Altus says it was angels," said Reginald. It sounded dumb when he heard the word pass his lips, but he had nothing left. Brian simply wasn't listening.

Brian gave a huge belly laugh. "This is from Altus? No surprise there. He's a *superstitious* asshole. All incubi are. They think they're demons; did Maurice tell you that?"

"Yes. But listen…"

"My youngest kid still believes in the tooth fairy. She's as dead serious about it as Altus is about angels and demons and Heaven and Hell. Maybe the tooth fairy destroyed the Council."

"Look, I'm not saying that it was literally…" Reginald began. But at that moment, in the background, someone began shushing the assembly, which meant that the proceedings were about to start.

"We should go up to the Deacon's box," said Maurice. He nodded a goodbye to Brian, who tipped them both a salute.

Maurice led the way from Council chamber, up a hidden set of stairs, into a boxed-off area in the stands. A chill ran through Reginald. He'd seen this place before, from below, from the floor of the arena, when he'd been on trial for his life. It was as if he'd gone back in time, and he and Maurice were stepping into the bodies of other people. Maurice would be playing the part of Logan, the Deacon he'd deposed. Reginald would be playing Logan's Deputy, who in Reginald's mind's eye was constantly making notes on a clipboard. Both were dead now, of course, and Reginald wanted to knock on wood and tell himself that history wasn't about to repeat itself. Maybe Brian had lost his fear of death, but Reginald certainly hadn't. It was being unfit that did it, he supposed. Maybe the Brians and Maurices and Charleses of the world had become predators, but Reginald still felt like prey.

And prey, by instinct, was always looking for the threat. He could feel it now. Just two weeks ago, this same building — in a different location — had been ripped apart by someone or something, and none of the milling vampires below him seemed to care. It was just business as usual for them. They had laws to pass, bigotry to spread. But Reginald could feel the threat hanging in the air, as if it was about to happen again.

He shook it off. Obsessing would help nothing right now.

Beside Maurice, in the box, was a large chair, like a throne. The throne was made of what looked like sandstone. That was another thing that was different from when Reginald had been here as a prisoner. Back then, the throne had been made of carved wood. Maurice had exposed the wooden throne as a safety hazard when he'd shattered it from behind, sending miniature wooden stakes into Logan's heart.

At the fore of the box, standing in front of of the throne, was Charles Barkley. He was rapping a stone against the arm of the chair and calling for order.

"Charles," said Maurice.

Charles looked back and smiled. He continued rapping the stone. "Order!" he said.

"That'll do, Charles," said Maurice.

"Order! This meeting of the Vampire Council is called to order!"

"Give me the stone and go back to the Council room, *Councilman* Barkley."

"Who are you and where is the Deacon?" said Charles, smiling vaguely.

"Last chance, Charles. I'm asking nicely."

"I'm doing you a favor here. They don't know who you are, Maurice. *Deacon* Maurice…"

"Deacon *Toussant*."

"… but they do at least know me. Now, if some stranger suddenly shows up in the Deacon's box claiming the Deaconship — some *small* stranger, say — then…"

There was a blur and a breeze as Maurice moved to Charles's side and deftly broke his neck. He turned Charles's head so far that it ended up facing backward, the skin on his neck ripped all the way around like a bloody necklace. Charles screamed, and that did finally bring the noisy room to order.

Maurice took the stone from Charles's hand and said, "Go back to the Council chamber, Charles."

"This *REALLY FUCKING HURTS!*" yelled Charles.

"By the common stairway, of course," said Maurice. "The rear stairway is for the Deacon and his staff only." He nudged Charles toward the front of the box where a long, meandering set of steps weaved through the bleachers before wrapping back to where Charles would be able to access the Council box.

Charles was trying to turn his head back around, but the muscles seemed to have torn. He grabbed both sides of the backward-facing head and tried to torque it back to front, but there was a snap and he stopped.

"You interlocked my vertebrae, you *ass*hole," said Charles, tugging at his head with both hands. Watching him was bizarre. Reginald honestly wondered which way he'd walk — forward blind, or backwards and at least be able to see?

"Suck it up, Charles," Maurice hissed. "Do you want a Snoopy band-aid for your boo-boo?"

"You could burn for this," said the back of Charles's head.

"I doubt it. I'm the Deacon. Right, Deputy?"

"'Deacon may injure Council members at Deacon's

discretion,'" said Reginald, making a note on a clipboard he'd found on a shelf at the back of the box.

Charles began to carefully make his way (backward for the torso and forward for the head) toward the large stairway. Maurice gave him a kind warning to watch out lest he break his neck on the way down.

When Charles was gone, Maurice grabbed the rock and banged it on the arm of the throne.

"I, Deacon Maurice Toussant, hereby call to order this meeting of the Vampire Council, yada yada yada, you get the idea," he said, a surprising amount of authority radiating from his small frame. "I know a lot of you here don't like that I'm here. But as the ancient human expression goes, *tough shit*. I am your Deacon, and you will show me respect. You don't have to like me. You don't have to support me. But the next person who fails to recognize my authority to lead this Council, having bested the previous Deacon as is our law —" He gestured at Charles, who tripped and fell as if on key. "— will be summarily staked. Do any of the rest of you want to challenge me? I'll face you one-on-one. Speak now or forever hold your petty comments."

He paused, his chest full and his head high. The room remained still.

"No? None of you who have challenged me in my absence? Who have questioned my right to rule or the presence of my proxy? None of you whom I've heard call me a relic, a throwback, a reactionary revolutionist? I know who you are, so speak if you're going to speak."

Reginald coughed.

"Fine," said Maurice. "Then as Deacon, I..." He trailed off, then looked over at Reginald.

"What?"

"I don't know how to conduct a Council meeting," Maurice whispered.

"You're supposed to have the Deputy read the minutes first. That's me. I don't know the minutes. I wasn't here and haven't reviewed the videos yet."

"Make something up," said Maurice.

Reginald walked to the front of the box. Someone laughed. Two or three voices muttered something.

"Minutes of the last meeting," said Reginald. "Council talked about laws. Then the building blew up."

The crowd increased its murmuring. Yes, they seemed to remember it that way too.

"Also, Charles Barkley was accused of fornication with a poodle. Charges were forgiven."

No objections came. Reginald wondered what else he could get away with, but decided not to push his luck.

"So are the minutes," said Reginald, concluding as he'd seen past minutes concluded in the records. Then, for effect, he bowed.

Reginald walked back to Maurice and whispered, "Now you make an opening address. Think Carson's opening monologue."

"I didn't prepare one."

"I just told them Charles screwed a poodle. I don't think it matters what you say," Reginald whispered.

"Can I talk about anything?"

"Sure. But I'd go for a rant. Openers are the time you get to speak without being interrupted by the Council."

Maurice stood up and walked to the front of the box.

"You are all assholes," he began. He looked back at Reginald.

"Maybe take it down a notch," said Reginald, holding his finger and thumb pinched together in front of his face.

Maurice turned back to face front.

"By which I mean that you're shortsighted. You refuse to see what's in front of your faces. You're a population that has entered into a willing, deliberate evolutionary bottleneck in order to become homogenous, with zero diversity in your population. There is, no pun intended, no new blood in our ranks. You must see that, yet you seem so intent on proving me and my ways wrong that you're willing to doom all of us to do it. I've been watching the new legislation. I've seen what's on the roster for tonight, and for meetings to come. Councilman Barkley has been pushing for an age limit for new vampires. The age is lower for women than men. Why would that be? I've seen the law that would require retroactive testing for vampires who are old enough to have never gone through the application and bootcamp process. What's the point? Any vampire old enough to fit that description would be orders of magnitude stronger than any new vampire. You are spinning your wheels in order to prove your own idiotic, asshole point. Two weeks ago, nearly four hundred among you died, and today you're back here not to talk about what happened and what it could mean and what to do, but to throw more… *asshole* legislation onto the docket because you don't like my ways and what I represent."

He paused. When it seemed that he was done — and not a bad opener, thought Reginald — a voice spoke up from the assembled audience.

"Permission to address the Deacon," it said. The speaker was a young man with jet black hair, severe black eyebrows, and a chiseled jaw.

Maurice nodded.

"All due respect, Deacon, but this isn't about being disrespectful. It's about quality control."

"Really," said Maurice.

"We survive on fear and spectacle. Humans outnumber

us a hundred thousand to one. They own the daylight. We need to be worthy of their fear and respect. Times are only getting harder. Humans are slowly covering and exposing every corner of the planet. If our representatives are…" He gestured in Reginald's direction. "I'm just saying, I don't know how frightened I'd have been, when I was human, of… of…"

"You can say it," said Reginald. "Of me. Of a fat guy."

The kid shrugged.

"How old are you?" said Maurice.

"Six years as a vampire."

"So, a child of modern cinema. Tell me: Before you knew we were real, how would you have described a vampire?"

"Uh…"

"Go ahead. You may speak freely."

"Fast. Strong. You killed them with a stake. They backed away from crosses and holy water. Maybe they flew. They were dark and glamorous. Sexy. Beautiful."

"Did becoming a vampire fix your flaws? Make you — as you said — dark, glamorous, sexy, and beautiful?"

"Yeah, for sure."

"Did you see *Nosferatu*?" said Maurice.

"Pardon?"

Maurice looked up from addressing the kid in the stands and played his gaze over the entire Council and assembly.

"You like to think that you're so different from humans," he said. "But you aren't. Few of you are older than one hundred years old. I am over two thousand. Throughout most of my life and through early cinema, vampires were monsters. Creatures of the night. Outcasts — and not in a brooding, fashionable way. In a 'we must

42

pursue and kill it' way. Vampires have not always been beautiful, sexy, and glamorous. We've been like goblins and ghosts. Things that were fearful because we were so *unlike* humans, not because we conformed so clearly to their ideals. I had a friend who was turned after losing most of his face, having been dragged half a mile over stone roads by his horse. Name was Jean. Nice guy. He didn't sparkle, but he scared the hell out of his victims. But there aren't many Jeans anymore. There's nobody like him, and supposedly it's all about 'quality control.' You grew up believing what you believed because it was what others showed to you, not because it was 'true.' You are slaves to pop culture. *Human* pop culture. The ideals you're striving for are not objective absolutes. They are new inventions. Your 'quality control' is actually just fashion."

"This reminiscing is nice," said a voice from the Council. If Reginald didn't know better, he'd swear the speaker was Todd Walker. "Can we move it along?"

Maurice threw up his hands. "Fine."

The crowd murmured. Reginald watched them, trying to read the room's mood. It was jovial. They'd already forgotten what Maurice had said… or, more likely, they'd never heard it.

"Good monologue," said Reginald. "Wrong crowd."

"Maybe the roof will come off again," Maurice said.

"One can hope."

"What do I do next?"

Reginald looked at the clipboard, flipping a page. He made a face.

"What?" said Maurice.

"Executions," said Reginald.

FIVE

Crazy Old Motherfucker

"It's a light night for executions," said Reginald. "Just one guy to execute."

"Then what?"

"Then it goes to new business, and the Council will begin voting in the new laws you just said were stupid."

"I'll get my veto stick ready. They can keep lobbing them in and I'll just keep hitting them out of the park."

"For now," said Reginald. "But they're starting to outsmart you. They're adding riders."

"Riders?"

"Apparently I've gone from one stupid system of government to another," said Reginald. "I'm a bit unclear, but it seems that vampire politicians can make mash-up laws just like US politicians can. One law might contain two prime parts to it. For now, the Council seems to just be playing around to see how you'll veto or not veto, but this could turn into an effective way to surpass the Deacon's veto power."

"What do you mean?"

"Like, one bill might contain legislation to prevent the eating of babies, and also impose an age restriction on bootcamp applicants. Since you can't make laws, you have the simple choice of allowing baby-eating or allowing the age restriction."

"They can't do that, can they?"

"I'm not totally sure, but it seems so." Reginald had read the text of all of the night's proposed laws while Maurice had been speaking. He'd also leafed through a rudimentary law book he'd found on the shelf. When he got home, he'd need to consult the official statutes online. He couldn't get an internet data signal on his phone from inside the building, because it was designed with jamming equipment.

"That's idiotic," said Maurice.

"That's government. Like I said, they're finding ways to outsmart you."

"Shit."

"It's okay," said Reginald. "I can outsmart *them*."

Maurice took a deep breath. "Okay. One step at a time. Let's deal with this execution. What's the guy's crime?"

"Wanton creation."

"Receiving? Or giving?"

Maurice was asking if the man was a vampire who'd been created illegally (like Reginald) or a vampire who'd created another illegally (like Maurice). Both were bad, and unless the new vampire could pass a strenuous test and be retroactively certified as acceptable, both maker and made could end up facing a death sentence.

"Receiving. He turned himself in, actually. Does that happen often?"

"It never happens," said Maurice. "It's not like we have

45

a downtown police station that new vampires can walk into. What do you mean, 'He turned himself in'?"

Reginald had already replaced the clipboard, having read the entire night's business. He would be able to recite it word for word, letter by letter, forever.

"He claims not to know his maker. Woke up with blood around his mouth, recalling none of the night prior."

"Glamoured. Glamoured *while* being turned, because it wouldn't be possible once he was fully vampire."

"Yes," said Reginald. "He knows who he is and what he is, but he's been figuring it out as he goes. He didn't realize it was a crime to exist, and here he is." Reginald found he was unable to keep the sympathy out of his voice. It was too easy to relate to the man.

"And he's already been tested and failed, because this shows up as an execution," said Maurice.

"Half right," said Reginald. "According to the paperwork, he's waived his right to a test."

"That's insane."

Reginald, who'd been through the test and had failed miserably, didn't think it was insane at all. He respected the man for trying to preserve his dignity.

"I'll just pardon him," said Maurice after a beat.

"The Guards say he's strange," said Reginald. That hadn't come off of the clipboard. He'd heard it when they'd passed a pair of Guards in the hall.

"I don't care how strange he is," said Maurice. "Two can play the game of 'let's do things just to piss off the opponent.' He's getting a big, fat pardon. Bring him in."

Reginald communicated Maurice's order to a member of the Guard, who ran off.

Moments later, a door slid open at the far end of the arena and Reginald felt his skin crawl. It was where he himself had been brought in five months earlier.

The crowd gasped.

The man who came through the door — with a burly member of the Council Guard on either side — had the face of a hawk. There was no other way to say it. He was at least seventy or eighty human years old with stark white hair and piercing eyes that Reginald could feel on him even from a distance. His eyebrows were pointed down his beaklike nose. Every vampire had a strength, and everything in the man's hawklike appearance said that his would be sight. He'd be able to spot a buttonhole from high orbit.

The prisoner flicked his head around the gathering like a bird. The spectators he looked at shrank back into their seats. It was a strange thing to see vampires do. Or rather, it wasn't strange at all. It was what legend said happened when vampires looked on crosses — a myth Reginald still hadn't tested.

"This man is a vampire?" said Maurice.

"Yes," said Reginald. Ever since Nikki had infiltrated the Council as a human, the Guard had begun testing every prisoner to make sure.

"He must be seventy."

"According to the file, he's ninety-three," said Reginald.

"He wouldn't have had a chance if I weren't here," said Maurice. Then he exhaled and shook his head. "I wish they'd brought someone in who wasn't quite so... unusual."

"No kidding."

"When I pardon a man this old..."

"They hate you already, Maurice," said Reginald. "And remember, you wanted to prove a point anyway."

"What's his name?"

"Thomas Balestro."

47

Maurice walked to the front of the box to address the old man just as Logan had during Reginald's trial, but the Guard hadn't yet released him. By this point in Reginald's trial, he'd already been tossed into the center of the arena and the Guard had walked out. Reginald also hadn't been bound in silver, and this man was heavily bound — far more than seemed necessary.

"Thomas Balestro," said Maurice. "I am Maurice, Deacon of this Council, and it is my duty today to assess you. You have waived your right to a physical trial. You won't be tried. You are pardoned. Go in peace."

But the Guards on either side of the man didn't move, didn't release his arms. Finally, the one to Balestro's right said, "Uh… Deacon? You may want to try this one."

"He's waived his trial. And he's pardoned," repeated Maurice. "You can all deal with an old vampire. Old, fat… we take all comers these days."

There was a grumble that ran through the stands at Maurice's pronouncement.

"Deacon?"

The same Guard. Maurice raised an eyebrow.

"That's not what I meant. I meant, he's unusual."

"He's old."

"He's *unusual*."

Maurice shook his head.

"He knew our names. He knew our family's names."

That wasn't anything special. Reginald knew the men's names and the names of their families, too. He also knew where they lived, what they'd been like as humans, how they'd been turned, which schools they'd gone to, what their parents occupations had been, and where they went on vacation. Before his trial, he'd read everything available on the Council and the Guard, then had scoured records and encrypted databases to find out all he could about everyone he could. You never knew when information might come in handy.

"Fine," said Maurice. "Unchain him and leave him."

The Guards remained where they were. This time, the other spoke.

"Um... Deacon? New procedure is to keep prisoners bound with silver, except during their actual testing, until their final release from the final set of escorts," said the Guard.

There had to be thirty pounds of silver chain on the man. It was absurd.

"Fine. You can go."

"And new procedure is for Guard to stay by prisoners until the trial commences."

"He's waived his right to trial."

"If you want to ask him questions, that counts as trial."

"Fine. Trial is commenced. Whatever gets you to leave." Then, to the prisoner: "This is just a formality. I'm sorry. And I'm sorry that this is how you're being welcomed into our society."

"I don't mind, Deacon," said the prisoner. "You may try me." He spoke with an accent that Reginald couldn't place. It was so subtle. English? Italian? French?

"Go," Maurice said to the Guards.

"Will there be a physical trial, Deacon?"

"Jesus."

"If there's no physical trial, we have to leave him bound," said one of the Guards, gesturing at the chains.

"I don't mind remaining bound," said Balestro.

"Whatever. Just leave." Reginald saw Maurice's arm flinch and realized that he'd just barely restrained himself from throwing the rock on the arm of the throne at the Guards out of sheer exasperation.

The two Guards nodded and backed away, keeping an eye on the prisoner as if they expected him to explode.

Thomas Balestro stood alone in the center of the packed-clay floor of the Council arena, silver chains binding his wrists and ankles, draped around his waist and over his shoulders. He didn't look very old to Reginald. He was supposedly ninety-three, but he wasn't stooped and there was nothing humbled in his eyes or his expression. He'd looked seventy when the Guard had brought him in, but now Reginald decided he'd place his age closer to sixty. His eyes bore the stare of an ambitious, aggressive man in his twenties. Reginald had seen the same stare from almost every twenty-something-seeming member of the audience and Council since they'd arrived.

Maurice turned to Reginald and whispered, "He's supposed to test while he's wearing all that silver? I couldn't climb a staircase with that much on me."

"They said it comes off for a physical trial. I'm guessing human Sub-Guards would come in and remove it. It's too much for the vampire Guards to handle."

"This is because of you?"

"Looks that way," said Reginald, who couldn't help but be flattered that he'd made the Council this paranoid.

And yet, the way the roof had come off two weeks earlier didn't seem to bother them at all.

Hard to protect against something you can't see — or something you don't believe in, he thought.

Maurice was ranting. "It's idiotic. If someone is a big enough threat to require that much silver, the threat will just be a threat again as soon as it's all removed."

"No," said Reginald. "Look."

Reginald pointed to a ring of windows above the stands that hadn't been there during his own trial. One advantage of a meeting place that was disassembled and reassembled every 8-10 days was that it was simple to make changes to the structure — such as adding a ring of sniper windows.

Reginald and Maurice looked around the edge of the arena, taking in the small windows. Each appeared to be made of thick, unbreakable Lexan. There was a tiny hole in each window, and the muzzle of a rifle protruded through each hole. Reginald had read about the security upgrade a few months ago. The rifles fired wooden bullets. Originally, the Council had considered placing archers at the windows, but missed arrows could be used as weapons. Bullets, on the other hand, were useless without the rifles that fired them.

"Again," Maurice said to Balestro, "I apologize for the chains."

"I understand completely. *I'd* keep me in chains if I were you," Balestro said mildly.

Maurice's face registered a puzzled expression.

"I'm a *baaaaad* man," said Balestro. "For instance, I'm about to kill a whole bunch of you."

Maurice turned to Reginald. "What else do you know about this man?"

"Nothing." Reginald's entire dossier on Thomas Balestro began and ended at the one-page affidavit he'd found on the shelf at the back of the Deacon box.

"Murder among vampires is serious business, Mr. Balestro," said Reginald. "I'd advise you not to joke about it. If I weren't here today, you'd probably already have been executed. Just so you understand the mood of this audience."

"Just making conversation," said Balestro. "Conversation such as the fact that this incestuous little community of yours has proven that absolute power does indeed corrupt absolutely, meaning that your deaths mean very,

very little. Well, *imagined* 'absolute' power, anyway. But yes, let's talk. What should we talk about? How about your wife, Deacon? Celeste. Yes. Lovely woman. Did you know that she had an affair a few years ago? Naughty naughty."

Balestro smiled a grin that was all teeth. Beside him, Reginald could see something change in Maurice's expression.

"But *you*, Mr. Baskin," he said, looking at Reginald, "you're who interests me most of all. The man who proved to the mighty Vampire Nation that brains mattered as much as brawn. And then you took your place beside the Deacon, fat and unfit to exist in the eyes of most. Tell me, how does it feel to have proven yourself as superior and more evolved... yet still be considered unworthy to live?"

For the first time in months, Reginald found himself outmatched. He had nothing to use against the man, and he couldn't read him at all. What did he want?

"I *want* to know what you think, Reginald," he said, as if he'd read Reginald's mind. "May I call you Reginald? I'd be honored if I could. Meeting you, after all, is one of the reasons I came here. Well, that and to kill a lot of vampires and to... well, the rest is a secret." He pressed his lips together theatrically.

Maurice, finding his voice, said, "Who are you?"

"I'm a poor old man who was turned into a vampire illegally, but fortunately, I'm about to be pardoned by the Deacon. Lucky me."

Reginald was running through scenarios in his head. Just because the man was cruel, angry, and had a lot of information didn't mean that he was a threat. But there was more to it. Reginald didn't like the way Balestro didn't seem to be humbled by the silver chains binding him. He was standing tall, as if the chains were simply a part of his clothing. And there was still the matter of the last session's odd happenings to consider.

"I'm a friend to you, Reginald," said Balestro. "Or at least, I could be, for the time that all of you have left. I want to know what it's like to be so universally rejected, despite your clear superiority. I want to know how you feel about being scorned simply because you've had the audacity to join a club that you're not good enough for."

The room had stopped talking.

"You don't want to tell me? Perhaps your human friends Nikki and Claire would have thoughts on the matter. It's 1:04pm. Claire just finished lunch and is drawing in class while she should be paying attention. Nikki is bored, sitting in an airport in New York, waiting for her connecting flight back to Columbus. I'm sure either would be happy for the diversion I'd offer. Does it strike you as odd that out of your three true friends, two are human? But of course…"

"You should execute him," Reginald said to Maurice.

Balestro made a hurt face. "Well, look at that. Now you're the one condemning people for being who they are. Should I die because I'm different?"

"Yes," said Reginald.

Maurice, accustomed to trusting Reginald's judgment, made a Roman emperor's "thumbs-down" gesture. It wasn't in the Council script, but it felt right. The crowd made pleased noises. Reginald felt conflicted. Balestro had to go, but Reginald didn't like that he'd done something that pleased the crowd.

Below them, on the floor of the arena, Balestro was pulling the silver chains away with a mildly bothered air as if he'd just realized he was covered with spider webs. The links broke with popping sounds like small-caliber rifle fire. He snaked a finger under each of the thick wrist manacles and pulled. They snapped as if made of kindling. When he was done, with the silver chains in a pile at his feet, he ran his hands over his clothes as if to smooth out wrinkles.

There was a sharp sound from above, and the fabric of Balestro's jumpsuit popped over his chest, leaving a small spatter of blood above his heart. The sequence repeated twice more. Reginald looked to where the sound had come from and saw one of the snipers reloading his rifle. The others were alternately looking at Balestro and then Maurice, whose presence in Council suddenly seemed to matter after all.

Balestro brushed fussily at the holes in his jumpsuit, then looked up at Maurice and Reginald as if to say, *Can you believe how rude that was?*

Maurice looked up at the snipers, ready with their wooden bullets.

"Again," he said.

This time, all of the snipers fired. Balestro's chest erupted into dozens of tiny geysers of blood as dozens of wooden bullets entered his heart. The impacts made his shoulders jump, but he remained otherwise impassive, waiting for the assault to end. When it finally did end, Balestro spread his hands at Maurice: *Are you finished?*

Maurice vanished from the Deacon's box fast enough that Reginald couldn't see where he'd gone. Suddenly, he was down on the clay floor — literally *on the floor*, lying on his back about twenty feet from Balestro.

Then, as Reginald watched, Maurice leapt up in a blur and ran at Balestro. Balestro watched him with boredom on his face. Maurice hit an invisible wall and flew back again, landing in roughly the same spot as before. Then, undeterred, he got back up and walked forward. He stopped a few feet from Balestro, but his toes continued to push into the dirt without actually moving him closer. It was as if he were being held at a distance by an invisible hand.

Reginald recognized the phenomenon. He'd experienced it himself when he first met Claire, when he tried to enter her house without her permission.

"What is this?" said Maurice.

"Checks and balances," said Balestro. "We had to give the humans something."

Maurice stepped back. From where Reginald stood, Maurice didn't look like the two-thousand year old Deacon of the Vampire Council. He looked like the teenager he must've once been, millennia ago.

"You have gotten used to the idea that you are on top," said Balestro, addressing the crowd. "But you are not."

Balestro's form flinched as if a tiny shiver had run through him. In the same instant, the heads of the entire front row of spectators became detached from their shoulders, and then, seconds later, both heads and torsos exploded into ash. Balestro was scratching at the side of his face before the last head hit the floor. Someone screamed. It was chilling to hear a vampire scream.

Balestro hadn't moved, and hence hadn't killed those vampires. And yet, he had.

"You have thirty days to quail in fear and decide whether you choose to die by our hand or your own," said Balestro.

"What do you…?" Maurice began.

"At midnight on the thirtieth day," said Balestro, interrupting him. Then he winked at Reginald. "*You'll* know where to find me."

Balestro crouched and exploded upward, propelled like a rocket toward the arena's metal ceiling. When he broke through it and into the bright mid-afternoon sun, the roof made an undramatic *foomp* sound. Then there was no Balestro, and there was only a shaft of sunlight spearing the pile of silver chains like a starlet in the spotlight. Maurice took a quick step back, away from the sun, and the spectators started to scream.

The rest of the meeting, including Charles's new legislation, was shelved for the time being.

SIX

Myths

It felt oddly normal, after a day of such incredible abnormality, to be at the office.

Maurice and Reginald were tired. They'd barely slept after a few hours of detention at the Council, four rides in blacked-out SUVs, and an insomniac day of indecision spent on and off the phone with Brian Nickerson, who'd stayed at the Council following what Reginald was already calling "the Balestro affair."

Nikki had arrived on a flight from New York a few hours earlier. She'd taken the whole week off and wasn't supposed to return to work until Monday, but she came in Friday night anyway because she missed Reginald and Maurice — and, as she'd explained months ago, she "had few friends among the living anymore." Nikki had almost been approved to become a vampire before Reginald's trial, and the coup had slowed things down enough that she was just now almost approved again. For six months, she'd been on the brink of leaving daylight forever, and had severed most of her daytime relationships accordingly.

Reginald was glad to have Nikki back. He wasn't used to having a girlfriend, and he'd missed her. He certainly wasn't used to having a *super-hot* girlfriend. He kept pinching himself. Then he'd pinch her. Then she'd pinch him. Then she'd try to get him, yet again, to have sex, because as she explained, "a girl has needs." But for six months, Reginald had demurred. It was hard to get his mind past the many years of rejection, he said. And so, reluctantly, she'd given him time to face whatever internal demons he still faced.

The atmosphere of the office was comforting, despite the fact that the day shift was having its annual customer appreciation event out in the main office space. Reginald, Maurice, and Nikki, who worked the night shift, hadn't been invited. This was fine with all three of them. Reginald loathed the day shift except for the three other misfits he never saw anymore — Sarah, Noel, and Scott, who of course wanted nothing to do with the annual customer appreciation event and had stayed home. Maurice didn't particularly like the day shift. Nikki was constantly warding off sleazy come-ons from the day shift.

And as far as the day shift was concerned, the trio represented another race, from another planet. The night shift workers, officially uninvited, would simply keep working while the event was going on. But it was Friday night, and most of the gym buyers were exactly like Walker, who was exactly like Berger, who was exactly like everyone else on the sales staff. So the party got drunk. And then it got loud. And then it spilled out of the conference room and across the cubicles, and Reginald, Nikki, and Maurice retired to the mail room, which seemed relatively safe.

Yet the presence of humans felt good, even though neither Maurice nor Reginald felt the need to feed at the moment. Humans were so normal. So harmless. What could a human do to you, compared to the awesome power that Balestro wielded?

Nothing, if you wore chain mail.

"You really are a genius, Reginald," said Maurice, admiring Reginald's chain mail shirt.

"No I'm not," said Reginald. "The rest of you are stupid. Think about it. Only three things will kill a vampire. Humans aren't able to pull off heads and sunlight doesn't come out at night. That leaves wooden stakes through the heart. Yet you never hear of vampires wearing simple chain mail shirts. You can't get a stake through chain mail. Hell, wooden bullets wouldn't even penetrate it. I can't believe nobody thinks of it."

The idea had seemed obvious to Reginald from the beginning, but the challenge turned out to be actually finding the chain mail. He'd looked at Army stores, speciality stores, hardware stores, and online, where he'd found only flimsy costume chain mail. Eventually he'd located the real thing, but the chain mail he discovered was the size of an XL shirt. When Reginald asked about size 4XL chain mail, the man on the other end of the phone told him that there hadn't been any fat knights. Reginald snapped back that he'd never heard of a fat vampire either, then hung up before the man could reply.

Eventually he'd ordered four chain mail shirts. He took two of them to a historical village and paid a blacksmith to have them combined into a giant chain mail parka big enough for — in the blacksmith's words — "Lancelot the Hut." The other two were in gift bags on the table.

"Yours is for later," Reginald told Nikki. "You know… for after you're turned."

"Can we do that tonight?" said Nikki, running a finger up Reginald's arm.

"Your re-authorization should come any day now. Let's wait and do it by the book, so that Maurice doesn't have to pardon you again."

"Good idea," said Nikki.

"Being executed would suck," said Reginald.

"*Suck*," Nikki repeated, removing her finger from Reginald's arm and placing it seductively between her lips.

"Dammit, Nikki, knock it off," said Maurice. Then, turning his attention to the remaining gift bag, he removed the chain mail and held it up to admire it. He pulled his shirt off, exposing a nineteen-year old, pimple-strewn, sunken chest. Then he pulled on the chain mail and put his shirt on over it.

Nikki had pulled off her own shirt and was standing next to them in a white bra that seemed very bright against her tan skin. She wiggled into the chain mail. Reginald told her that there was no point for her to wear it yet and tried to grab at it, but she smacked his hand away. Then she asked him if he'd seriously never worn a Halloween costume around the house before Halloween just because it was awesome.

When her shirt was back on, she bounced lightly on her toes and said, "This shirt is heavy."

"Take it off, then," said Reginald. Then he added, "Slowly."

"If only I had a pole," said Nikki.

"Writhe against the vending machine," Reginald suggested.

"I like vending machines," said Nikki, licking her finger. "If I push the right buttons, I can get nuts to pop out."

"Jesus, Nikki," said Maurice.

"I've been meaning to ask you," said Reginald, "were

you around for Jesus? I mean, you must've been, but did you know him?"

"That's like asking a guy from New York if he knows Derek Jeter," said Maurice.

"So you're saying Jesus was like Derek Jeter?"

"Maybe." He cocked his head. "Probably."

Then the door banged open and the bright white tombstone teeth of Todd Walker burst into the room. A pair of enormous breasts came with him.

Walker looked at Nikki, then Reginald, then Maurice. Then he said, "Hey look, it's the company vampires."

"Lucky guess," said Reginald.

"Ha ha!" said Nikki. "I get it. Because we work at night. You're hilarious. Are you here to have sex with this woman? Go ahead; we can scooch back a bit."

Walker's facial features went blank. The tombstone teeth vanished.

"Yes," said the woman with the enormous breasts. "Do you mind?"

Reginald crossed the room toward Walker and his conquest. He looked the woman in the eyes.

"You don't want to have sex with this man," he said. "You want to go back to the party and tell everyone that he begged and begged, but that you were disgusted by him. So he paid you to have sex. You were willing to do it, but when you saw the size of his penis, you laughed so hard that you lost your balance and fell forward into said penis, knocking Walker here into that wall over there. Then an open printer ink refill fell from the shelf and coated his penis in red ink. Because of this, months from now, everyone will be calling him, 'Ol' Red Dick.'"

The woman looked back into Reginald's eyes and said, "Sure."

Maurice didn't tell Reginald that he couldn't glamour

the woman and expect behavior out of other people as he had in the past. *Any* vampire could command a person to do things themselves, but Reginald was a glamouring virtuoso. He could influence people to influence *other* people. Reginald's instructions to humans were always vague, trusting their subconscious minds to fill in the specifics.

Reginald looked at Walker. "You'll help her prepare and then will forget everything that happened in this room tonight," he said.

Walker nodded, and then the drama began to take shape.

Walker stood several feet from the wall he'd supposedly been run into, then ran backward at it and rammed the wall with his rear in order to leave a convincing ass-hole in the drywall. Plaster poofed out in a tiny cloud. Then Walker and the woman found a vial of red printer ink, spattered it on Walker's pants and on the floor below the shelf, and then tossed the bottle into a corner. The woman mussed her hair, and they walked out.

"Will it literally be 'Ol' Red Dick'?" said Maurice, fascinated.

"Yes. Human minds are like locks. They are very easy to open once you see the pattern. I planted an idea in her mind, and she'll plant ideas in the minds of a few of the others outside. In fact, they'll probably think the nickname was their idea."

There was a crash from outside the door, and the sound of the party increased. There was much hooting and hollering. Even through the door, Reginald could hear Walker called a "douche" at least twice.

Then, relative quiet returned to the closed mail room. There was something in the air — something heavy and unspoken.

"Maurice," said Reginald.

Maurice looked over.

"Do vampires have an explanation for themselves?"

Maurice shook his head. "What do you mean?"

"I mean that you all act so rational, like you're above believing in the 'superstitious crap' that Altus believes. I couldn't figure out why that bothered me, but then I realized what was going on: *You're just being human.* Once upon a time, we were *all* human, and even now, as vampires, we live in the middle of a human culture. Sensible humans believe in rationality and science and observable phenomena, and sensible vampires believe the same. But sensible humans also don't believe in *us*, Maurice, and they don't believe in incubi and succubi. It's like vampires have taken this very rational frame of beliefs and have said, 'The humans are right that magic and supernatural stuff is bullshit... oh, except that there are vampires.' So I was just wondering — do vampires have a rational, scientific explanation for themselves so that they can explain away the fact that magic doesn't fit into their sensible worldview?"

"Is this about angels?"

"Angels. Demons. Heaven. Hell. You laugh at it all like you'd laugh at the Easter Bunny, but *the mere fact that you exist* should cause you to at least open your mind to those possibilities. You are a counterexample to your own argument that everything should be explainable and sensible."

Maurice drummed his fingers on the table. "It's not that simple," he said.

"Sure it is. History is filled with discoveries of unknown and impossible things. Someone realizes that crazy things exist or figures them out, and then everyone accepts them. If aliens landed on the White House lawn tomorrow, people wouldn't throw out their entire system of beliefs. They'd simply fit aliens into that system of beliefs and would make a small amendment: 'Okay, aliens aren't ridiculous anymore, but this *other* stuff is still obviously impossible and ridiculous.'"

Maurice shook his head. "It's so deep. So deep in our mythos."

"Then tell me," said Reginald.

"Yeah, Maurice," said Nikki, propping her elbows on the table. She had an interest in mythology that bordered on a fetish. Reginald had made fun of her because she'd taken a 3-volume compendium of the Greek gods with her on vacation.

"All right," said Maurice. "To answer your question — Do we have an explanation for ourselves? — the answer is yes and no. We don't have a rational explanation, no. We don't know what makes us tick, really, and we don't know, actually and precisely speaking, who the first vampire was. There are two basic schools of thought on it. One says that vampires and humans co-evolved as separate species and that we had our own 'mitochondrial Eve,' and one says that humans came first and that we evolved from them in a way not unlike a certain famous fish crawled out of the ocean and breathed air one random day.

"But on the other side of 'do we have an explanation?' — yes, we do. On the non-rational side, we have a myth.

"Now, two things you need to understand about vampire myths. The first is that even though we tell the stories, we don't actually *believe* them. It's like how some Native Americans talk about the world being created when a beetle came down from the sky, found nothing but water, and dragged mud up from the bottom of the ocean so he'd have a place to stand. They, like us, don't literally believe those myths today, but they tell them anyway. It's part of their culture.

"But the second thing to understand is that unlike with Native Americans, our myths aren't told from parent to child. Vampires are, almost all of the time, turned willingly when they're adults. That skews our demographics. Most people who apply to become vampires do so because they're damaged in some way." His eyes flicked to Nikki, who looked down. "No offense, Nikki. But below the surface, most vampires — at least today — are emotionally disturbed, or angry, or grew up powerless and now want power more than anything. You're choosing a life of eternal youth that revolves around ritualistic, sexualized behavior. You're choosing never to see the daytime again, to live in shadows and indoors, and to be a predator and a killer. And now think: Our myths spread from jaded, damaged adult to jaded, damaged adult. There is no innocence or blind acceptance. Everyone knows the myths, and while nobody believes them, they'll often talk themselves into believing parts of them because it gives them *purpose*."

Maurice looked into Nikki's eyes, Reginald's eyes.

"If I could psychoanalyze a little bit, vampires are lost souls," he said. "Humans at least have pervasive myths in their culture about where they came from and where they're going, but what about us? We start as directionless, jaded people. We make a conscious choice to turn away from our humanity, and after that, in the big picture, we're given no direction. We live forever, so there's no need for an afterlife. So what our myths do is to act as a glue and to fill that void in meaning. Vampires have to believe in something or they'll go mad, so they grab onto our myths. They laugh at them on one hand and embrace their core meanings on the other. But then, because they're approaching the myths as fully formed adults, they'll ritualize them, or subconsciously embody them, or use them as excuses for atrocities. Does that make any sense?"

Reginald, who knew of Maurice's interest in psychology, nodded.

"So with all that out of the way, the vampire creation myth — the one that nobody literally believes but that everyone tells — goes like this: In the distant, distant past, in the time of Adam and Eve, the universe was ruled by God and angels. Yes, the same god — at least in the modern version of the myth. A group of angels tried to seize power, were foiled, and then were cast out of Heaven. In some versions of the myth, Lucifer is one of these fallen angels, and in others he's not. In some versions there is a Hell, and in some versions there is not. But in all versions, there are six fallen angels, three of each gender — presumably anthropomorphized from our own genders — and they settle here, on earth, on the mortal plane, as the first earth-dwelling immortals.

"Now, God had already created Adam and Eve, and just like in the Christian tradition, they were his most treasured creations. But there was a problem. He had six very dangerous renegade angels to contend with, and he didn't trust them, as well he shouldn't. But the fallen, themselves, were between a rock and a hard place. God had thus far only banished them and could, they suspected, incinerate them instead. So a kind of detente grew between them — an acrimonious 'agreement to disagree,' say. But it was too tenuous. Neither side trusted the other. The angels feared being destroyed, and God feared for his creations.

"And so they negotiated, like divorced parents would negotiate over a child they share. They came to an agreement. Adam and Eve would have two sons: Cain and Abel. Cain and Abel would represent a branching of intelligent life on earth into two. In the human version of the myth, Cain kills Abel. In the vampire version, they both kill each other, over and over and over again. First Cain kills Abel. God resurrects Abel. Then Abel, furious, kills Cain, who is resurrected by the fallen angels. It goes on and on and on, brother killing brother, neither side willing to surrender. So eventually, the only way to keep them apart so that each can father his own branch of life on Earth is to 'sunder the day' and give each dominion over one. Abel is given the day, the light, and the spark of life. Cain is given the night, the darkness, and the dead."

"So when Altus talks about angels…" said Reginald.

"Correct. He's talking about these mythical Six."

"But why would they be against us? We're supposed to be in their corner, according to the myth."

Maurice shrugged.

"Maybe he's talking about other angels," said Nikki. "You know, the good ones."

"Does it matter?" said Maurice. "It's a myth."

"Just for the sake of argument."

"Vampires act like there are only those Six. Incubi too. You never hear anyone talk about any 'good angels.'"

"I just don't get it," said Nikki.

"Because it's a myth," said Maurice. "Do you believe that sky beetle dragged mud up from the ocean to make the land of the Earth?"

"But I still don't see why the angels would have supposedly turned on vampires," said Reginald.

Maurice rolled his eyes and stood up. "Magic coyote. They turned on us because a magic coyote came in and barked, and then the cactus spirit toked up some weed and the sky fell."

"Hey, you said yourself that vampires take these things into their psyches and 'use them as excuses for atrocities.' We've seen atrocities in the past two weeks. I think it's worth understanding."

"So you think Balestro was an angel."

"I don't know *what* Balestro was. But wouldn't you

agree that we're facing a very serious threat — no matter whether it's mortal, immortal, or angelic?"

Maurice shrugged and sighed, acquiescent.

"And we've been given a deadline, remember. Thirty days. 29 days now. Talk about ritualism. We don't have to believe any myths, but Balestro and anyone who might be with him seem to."

"So…"

"We've got to at least figure it out and decide how to respond," said Reginald. "Whatever Balestro was, he's bigger and better than us. I'd say there's a one hundred percent chance we'll regret it if he does come back and we've done nothing but sit around with our thumbs up our asses.

"So," he said to Maurice. "We should talk to Brian about manufacturing some consensus on the Council. Let's meet in my apartment tomorrow at midnight. In fact, have Brian drag Charles along. We'll have to get him involved. He's an ass, but he represents everyone who hates us. They won't listen to us, but they'd listen to him."

Maurice nodded, then peeked out the small window in the mail room door. He looked at the clock on the wall above Walker's ass-hole in the plaster.

"One fifteen," he said. Then he cocked a thumb over his shoulder, at the mail room door. "They're shitfaced out there and it's only going to get worse. Anyone want to knock off early for the weekend? They'll never know."

"Good idea," said Reginald, standing from his chair. "I have some reading to do anyway."

SEVEN

Diabeetus

Reginald was upside down, balanced on one hand in the center of his living room, when the doorbell rang.

He wasn't just doing acrobatics. He was multitasking. On the floor below him was a laptop, and on the laptop were the video records of the past two chaotic Council meetings. Reginald was also using the laptop to research vampire mythology, and was also using the hand to eat Doritos.

Getting into the handstand had taken a while. He'd stood in front of a wall, put his hands on the floor, and attempted to kick up. The first time he'd tried, he'd plowed his face into the ground. The second time, he'd rolled over and ended up wedged in the corner between the floor and the wall, and had to smash an end table to escape. The third time he'd kicked a giant hole in the wall.

But the fourth time, he'd suddenly and astonishingly found himself standing on his hands, his back against the wall, staring out into his upside-down living room. It was a strange sensation. As he held the position, he went back to that strange place in his mind where his vampire abilities resided. Something clicked. His muscles stopped trying, and simply did what they were supposed to do.

It dawned on him that handstands were easy. He wondered why he'd never realized it before.

Reginald's balance crawled upward from his hands to his core, from his core to his legs. He realized that his legs didn't matter. He alternatively let them hang and straightened them, watching his balance move with his mind's eye as if it were a ball of light in his center.

He walked away from the wall on his hands, into the center of the room. Maurice had been right; it didn't take much strength. He was just holding himself up, not flexing and extending muscles. So he picked one hand up off the carpet and held it out to the side, balancing on the other hand. He kicked his legs up into the air and made tiny hops. Then he tried the other hand.

Balance. Who knew?

He started to feel cocky.

He put both hands back on the floor and, looking down, his back arched, attempted to lower himself to the carpet for a handstand pushup. The carpet jumped up and hit him in the face like it was angry with him. As he fell, his feet punched another hole in the plaster.

Not yet on the handstand pushups, anyway.

So he'd gotten the laptop and had started studying, and that's when the doorbell rang.

Reginald carefully lowered his feet to the ground, placed the computer and a bag of Doritos he'd been eating one-handedly onto the coffee table, and opened the door. He found Charles Barkley in the doorway, levitating three inches off the ground.

Charles's whole body jiggled and, without moving his lips, Charles said, "Hi Reginald! I fuck poodles!" Then he flew into the room and crushed the coffee table. The computer was spared.

Behind him, the gigantic figure of Brian Nickerson stood with its arm out. Then the arm went down.

"'Sup, Reginald," he said.

"'Sup," Reginald echoed.

Once Brian cleared the doorway and moved to stand beside it, Reginald saw that Maurice and Nikki were behind him. Nikki had her arms crossed and was shivering.

"Are you cold?" Reginald asked.

"F-f-f-freezing," she said.

Todd Walker stepped around Nikki and sauntered uninvited into Reginald's apartment.

"Walker?" said Reginald.

Brian hit Walker hard on the back. Walker became Barack Obama.

"Altus," said Reginald.

"Reginald," said Barack Obama. Then Obama walked into the living room, sat on Reginald's La-Z-Boy chair, and put up the foot rest.

"Fuh-fuh-fuh," said Nikki.

"I'll get a sweater," said Reginald. He came back minutes later with a garment that Nikki vanished completely inside of, as if she'd wrapped herself with a blanket.

Reginald raised an eyebrow at Maurice.

"Hey," said Maurice, "you wanted a meeting of Heaven and Hell, so I figured I'd invite the only demon I know. Too bad he's a huge cock, but then again, he's a demon. It's how they roll."

"This place smells like human," said Charles, who'd extricated himself from the coffee table.

"Have a seat, dickbrain," said Brian.

Charles sat on the couch.

"Not there," said Brian.

Charles stood.

Brian motioned for Reginald to sit on the couch and then sat down beside him. Reginald felt sorry for the couch. Sitting side by side, Reginald thought that he and Brian must look like before-and-after photos for a fitness alchemy pill.

There were two chairs in Reginald's breakfast nook. Maurice and Nikki dragged them to the coffee table and sat in them, with Nikki bundled up like Nanook of the North. Charles looked around and, after a moment's indecision, sat down on a milk crate that Reginald sometimes used as a step stool.

"I'd intended to keep this reality-based and secular," said Reginald, "but now that Altus is here, I'm sure it'll devolve quickly."

"I don't have to be here, you know," said Barack Obama.

"Nonetheless, let's try to start with the facts, because I don't think anyone can argue with the facts. Fact One: In the middle of May, the roof came off of the Council building during a meeting of the Council and the general assembly. Nearly four hundred vampires died in the midday sun. There was no apparent reason for the roof to come off. Spotters outside the complex saw nothing, no equipment, no explosion, nothing. The cameras inside show no fire, no explosion, and no blurs of motion other than after things got rolling and everyone started running. For some inexplicable reason, the Council has more or less chosen to believe that this was somehow an accident, like maybe the roof wasn't screwed on tight and there was a lot of wind that day."

"It was a gas explosion," said Charles.

"No," said Reginald, "it very obviously was not. And

on a slightly different topic, I'd like to know why a few years as a vampire causes one to live with one's head firmly planted inside of one's ass. No offense, Brian." He was thinking of how Brian had scoffed at all of this the last time they'd spoken.

"You're right, Reginald," said Brian. "It's pretty obvious now that I've spent some time thinking. You just kind of get used to being on top. You start to believe what you want to believe. But after Balestro…"

"And that's Fact Two," said Reginald. "At the last meeting, Thomas Balestro, apparently a prisoner, breaks through thirty pounds of silver chain, creates a force field that a two-thousand-year-old vampire can't penetrate, is unhurt by wooden bullets through the heart, kills a dozen vampires without anyone seeing him move, and then flies through the roof and into the sun. By my count, that's six things that vampires can't do. So whatever Balestro is, he's not a vampire. Anyone have any doubt that everything I've just said is objectively true?"

"I know where this is going," said Charles.

"Any arguments *with the facts?*" Reginald repeated.

Charles made an unimpressed face.

"Look. Everyone here knows that Altus —" Reginald extended an arm toward Barack Obama. "— thinks that this is about angels, and I know how that sits with everyone, but try to divorce yourself from the 'obvious falsity' of the myth. Call him by whatever *name* you want, but whatever Balestro is, he's much more powerful than we are and can go out in the sun. He says he's coming back, and if he does, that's going to be very bad for those who are around. We've got to prepare."

"You can't prepare against angels," said Barack Obama.

"Just… forget 'angels' for a second," said Reginald,

waving an arm at Obama and addressing the others. "*Prepare*. Like, against a clear threat."

"Angels aren't a threat," said Obama. "'Threat' implies some chance of surviving it, which you don't have."

"See, this is why I wasn't going to invite him," Reginald said to Maurice.

"Screw you, I can go," said Obama.

"Good. Go."

"G-g-go," agreed Nikki, hugging the sweater tightly around herself.

"Maybe later," said Obama, suddenly transforming into Wilford Brimley.

"Prepare how?" said Brian.

"You'd know better than me," said Reginald. "Better security. Weapons. I don't know what you have. The only thing I know for sure is that it'll take more than the handful of us in this room. You two need to convince the Council, and the Council needs to convince the Nation."

"This is such crap," said Charles.

"You're totally nonplussed by Balestro, then? No surprises from that nutty old guy?"

"Trickery," said Charles. "Complicity of the guards. Anything could explain it. Fake chains. Jet packs. Shit, magnets. Anything but angels. If you're dealing with anything at all, it's a conspiracy. Something that we need to root out from within, not by making doomsday procla- mations."

"So what you're saying is that this is the work of vampires. Just… *normal vampires*."

Charles shrugged, thoroughly uninterested.

"Vampires who can go out in the sun," said Reginald.

"He wasn't a vampire," said Brian.

"Advanced genetic engineering," said Charles. "Some kind of a daywalker."

"He wasn't Wesley Snipes," said Maurice.

"You are all so *pitiful!*" said Charles. "Fat guys. Old guys. Fraternizing with humans and incubi." He tilted his head toward Nikki, then Altus. "You overthrow the government and expect to take it off in ridiculous new directions. But you can't, and that's why we have checks and balances. This... *whatever* it is... won't be your excuse."

Reginald's mouth fell open. "You think *we're* behind it," he said.

Charles scoffed.

"You do! You think Maurice and I are manufacturing an enemy to gain support in the Nation and on the Council. It's like Salman Rushdie and the Ayatollah Khomeini."

Charles said nothing.

"I'm flattered," said Reginald. "But you saw Balestro yourself. How do you explain what he could do? Jesus, get your head out of your ass for just a second and think about it."

Charles crossed his arms.

"Okay, then," said Reginald. "More facts. The Guard, assuming they weren't in on it, would have tested Balestro. They would have cut him and verified that he healed. They would have exposed him to pinpoint sunlight to see if he burned. They would have pulled on his fangs with pliers to be sure they were real. Could he *maybe* be a vampire? Could he just be *very* old and *very* strong and *very* fast?"

"No vampire — and especially not an old one — can survive that much direct sunlight," said Maurice.

"Unless he was so old that he represented a prior evolutionary step," said Brian.

"Or the *next* evolutionary step," said Nikki.

"He went out into sunlight at the end," said Brian.

75

"But that would mean that if he blistered when the Guard tested him earlier with sunlight, he'd have to be..."

"Shape-shifter," said Maurice, looking toward the La-Z-Boy.

"Hey, don't look at me," said Wilford Brimley. "We can't go out in the sun either. It's like the *diabeetus*."

"*And* you're weak and slow," Brian added.

"But we get all the girls." Wilford tossed back a head of imaginary elegant hair.

"There are no records of shape-shifters that strong or fast," said Reginald. "So it's something we've never seen before."

"Or something you collectively haven't seen in so long that you've forgotten," said Wilford Brimley.

Charles rolled his eyes.

"Okay," said Reginald, looking at Altus. "Might as well go there. Just for the hell of it, say he's an angel. He's one of the Six who made the deal with God to create vampire Cain and human Abel, and so on and so forth. What then?"

"You mean, what comes next if he has some sort of a grudge against all of you?"

"Yes."

"Then you're fucked."

"I meant, what do we do?" said Reginald.

"What you do is, you get fucked."

"The thirty-day thing, I mean."

"What about it?"

"'You have thirty days to quail in fear and decide whether you choose to die by our hand or your own.' What did that mean?"

"Oh, you meant that."

"Yes."

76

"And you want to know what it means, you having thirty days."

"Yes."

"Well," said Wilford Brimley, sitting forward in the recliner, "What that means is that you have thirty days."

"Right."

"And after those thirty days are up…" He pressed his forefinger and thumb together into the universal gesture of making a very specific and important point. "… *you're fucked*."

Brian sat up onto one buttcheek, leaned toward the recliner, and punched Altus in the stomach.

"Let's try that again," he said.

Altus, as Wilford Brimley, wheezed for breath. Reginald thought he might have said something again about the diabeetus.

"Look," said Altus. "What you've got to understand about angels and demons is that most of us are big on rituals, same as the human institutions that worship us on both sides of the good/evil coin. Lighting candles, dancing in circles, chanting, sacrifice. Just look at what they did with Cain — the thing with him walking the earth forever cursed because he'd struck first. They didn't have to do that. It was symbolic, to give Cain and his descendants a black mark for eternity. They create the hype, then they believe and abide by what they just created as if it were law. They'll burn people forever in sulfur because it's always been sulfur, despite the fact that Hell could easily have upgraded to magnesium, which burns much hotter and much cleaner and doesn't stink."

Brian: "And this has to do with…?"

"The thirty days. It's a ritual. Why give you time for… for whatever? Because once upon a time, they themselves decided arbitrarily that they should."

"And what are we supposed to do with the time?"

"Quail in fear, apparently," said Altus.

"He said something about a decision, though," said Reginald. "What are we supposed to decide?"

Altus nodded suddenly, as if something had just occurred to him. "The free will thing. I forgot. Free will is Heaven's one big check, its ace in the hole. It's also why angels can't see into the future — they can't understand free will. Angels can't *force* you to do anything because of it, or impose a defining action on you. Let's say an angel wants to kill you. Well, he can't just kill you; you have to *decide* to die. So the way the angel gets around it is, he gives you some kind of a choice. In this case, it's a redemption period. During that redemption period, you either do nothing or try to redeem yourself and fail. In either case, it's your actions or lack thereof that have caused you to die. Free will, see."

"That's like something a lawyer would pull," said Nikki. "It's so arbitrary."

"Well, the lawyers don't *all* go to Hell," said Wilford Brimley.

Reginald stood and faced Altus. "What happens if, during whatever free will trial you get, you manage to redeem yourself?" he said.

"You can't."

"But what if you…"

"You can't," Altus repeated. "Angels aren't humans. They aren't emotional. You're not going to impress them and make them cry by showing them a PBS moment wherein you save a puppy. They want you decimated, the decision is already made. The waiting period is a formality, nothing more."

Charles stood up. "I've had enough retardation for the evening. I'll be going now."

"You've got to talk to the Council," said Maurice.

"No," he said, "I don't." He looked over at Brian, who was rising from the couch. "Threaten me all you want," he said. "You haven't convinced *me*, so there's no way that I or anyone else will convince the Council. The Council disagrees with you on *principle*, Maurice. Even if you had a perfect case, which you don't, there is absolutely zero chance you'll derail the entire government and get the whole Nation to stop what it's doing, rally behind *you* of all people, and mass weapons that this dickhead says are useless anyway against some arbitrary threat from a story-book, in less than a month. And you know it."

Maurice shook his head. Charles made an *Are we done?* gesture. When nobody responded to it, he became a blur and was gone.

Wilford Brimley had moved into the kitchen while Charles was speaking.

"I could use some nutritious Quaker oatmeal," he said.

EIGHT

Chess

After Brian and Altus had gone, Nikki snuggled up next to Reginald on the couch. Maurice lit a cigarette. He dragged deeply on it, exhaled, and repeated. The room waited for someone to speak, but nobody did.

Reginald pulled a coin from his pocket and rolled it across his knuckles. After discovering his surprising new facility with balance, he'd begun looking for other abilities that might arise from better muscle coordination, and card and coin tricks seemed to be among them. Seeing a demonstration earlier, Maurice had said that Reginald would be an excellent pickpocket or card shark.

"We'll never convince Charles to do anything," said Reginald.

"And even if he did, the Council wouldn't listen," said Maurice. "It's so inconvenient to think that the world might end."

"This sweater smells like ham," said Nikki, as if the thought had just occurred to her.

"This is so strange," said Maurice.

"I know," said Nikki, smelling the sweater.

Maurice was tapping the eraser end of a pencil on the desk in front of him, pensive.

"What?" said Reginald.

"Just feel the mood in here," said Maurice. "I feel like we're bracing to survive a hopeless war, but all we have is one encounter with one guy who got the best of some of us. I hate to say it, but Charles's take on this is much more sensible."

"Maybe. But what if our take is the right one?"

"Our take? Does this mean you're committing to, 'A biblical angel is stalking vampire-kind?'"

"I know it sounds stupid, but..."

"But they're fairy tales," said Maurice.

Reginald leaned forward. "You want to hear a story, my friend?" he said. "I grew up believing *vampires* were fairy tales. Shape-shifters and incubi too."

"That's different."

"No, it's not. You know what it took for me to believe that vampires were real? I had to become one. Put me in a room a year ago with three humans and change this conversation so that we're talking about you — a guy who can be shot and heal instantly, who burns in the sunlight, who drinks blood and can live forever. We'd all be telling each other that you were wearing body armor, had a skin condition, and were a goth freak obsessed with the occult. You'd sprint around the room and lift a piano, and then as soon as you'd gone, we'd start saying how it must have been a trick of light, or we were hallucinating. Anything but the truth. Logan even said it back at my trial — the main reason humans don't know we exist is because they *refuse to believe it*."

"What are you saying?" said Nikki.

"I'm saying that if it looks like an angel, walks like an angel, and talks like an angel, we should start with *believing* it's an angel, not disbelieving it. It's not unscientific to believe a myth. What's unscientific is to refuse to believe something that all of the evidence is pointing toward simply *because* it's a myth. As you once told me, Maurice, let's be the first people to see what's right in front of our faces."

Maurice was shaking his head slowly, trying to find a way to agree with Reginald.

"The myth says that six renegade angels made a kind of Faustian bargain with God to create two races: vampires and humans. Vampires were given the night. Humans were given the day. Vampires were given speed and strength, but cursed with several mortal weaknesses, such as allergies to silver, wood, and sunlight. Humans were given the ability to protect the places they lived, and vampires couldn't approach without a deliberate invitation. Another interesting thing I discovered. Maurice, is it true that a human can't be glamoured into letting a vampire inside their home?"

Maurice laughed. "Yeah. Everyone eventually figures that out. It's a running joke with new vampires to not tell them and let them figure it out for themselves. Our version of hazing."

"Think about it. Why would that be? 'That human won't let me in? Fine... I'll force him to!' But you can't. It's too convenient, the way that loophole is closed. It seems to require a conscious choice — something intervening to keep the game fair for humans. It sounds like what Altus said: rules for the sake of rules. Ritual for the sake of ritual."

"You think it's a game?" said Nikki.

Reginald nodded. "I think it was a bet. A wager between what humans call God and what you call the Six. The genesis force of each race, pitting its players against each other. One dark and one light, like a giant game of chess."

Reginald looked at Maurice. "What Balestro did to you, keeping you away from him? That looked to me like the same magic that keeps vampires from entering human homes. Something, say, that his kind might have given to humans when it all began. But if that's true, it means that you couldn't touch him unless he allowed it, and I'd say that's a significant disadvantage in a fight — especially if they deliberately gave us weaknesses and know exactly what those weaknesses are."

Nikki began biting her fingernails.

"And there's free will again — humans choosing to let us in. Ritual. Rules. I always thought the things supernatural beings had to abide by seemed so arbitrary. Like the stake through the heart. Why would that hurt an immortal creature? Because once upon a time, someone said so."

"So what do you think all of this is?" said Maurice. "What did Balestro mean? What would he want?"

"Maybe the game is over," said Reginald. "Maybe the Six are tipping over their king on the big chessboard."

"Conceding defeat?" said Nikki.

"Why not? How many vampires are there in the world, Maurice?"

"At last census, around seventy thousand."

"Worldwide, or US?"

"Worldwide."

Reginald nodded. "Humans number nearly seven billion. I'd call that a loss for our side, and that despite our superior speed and strength."

Nikki hugged her arms around herself. "Ugh. I can't believe I've got a date to join the losing team right at the final buzzer. This almost makes me not want to become a vampire. *Almost*."

"Look," said Reginald. "It *could* be nothing, of course. But I think we should consider the possibility that we're facing a game-over situation. Maybe the powers that be are preparing to fold up the chess board, put away the black pieces, and let the winning team have the field to themselves."

"Why?" said Nikki.

"Maybe it was the terms of the bet," said Reginald. "There's a lot out there — fragments of myth that never made it down the line, through the aeons, into the version we know today. There are bits that talk about the angels' names, for instance. One of the Six was named Baelstrom, similar to our word 'maelstrom.' Do I need to point out what a maelstrom is, or how similar the name is to our guy? And there are allusions to a final countdown before armageddon, too. Consider it an overtime period, during which the losing side has a chance to continue playing. Sort of like how when you fail out of a video game, sometimes you'll get ten or twenty seconds to insert another coin and continue."

"I'll bet I can guess how long the overtime period was," said Maurice.

"A convenient way to measure things in the long-ago," said Reginald, nodding. "One moon. Now, technically, the lunar cycle is 29.53 days, so I guess they rounded up."

Nikki tapped her chin with a finger. "28 days left."

"The overtime period," said Maurice. "You said the losing side has a chance to keep playing?"

Reginald shook his head. "I doubt it. It reads like it's just more ritual. Technically we'd have a choice, but it sounds like a choice with no correct answer. You heard what he said. The choice isn't whether to live or die. The choice is whether to die by their hand or our own. It's a way out of the loophole, nothing more."

Maurice tapped the pencil eraser on the desk. Reginald made a coin vanish, appear, vanish.

"So is this it?" said Nikki. "You just do nothing and wait?"

"We can hole up. We can run. Or we can try to bargain."

"Bargain. How?"

Reginald shrugged. "Beg for our lives, maybe."

Maurice sat up straight. There was a small noise as the cigarette dropped from his fingers and hit the floor.

"Or," he said, "we could right the game."

Reginald, surprised to be caught off guard for a change, looked up at Maurice. "How?"

"Have you ever been to France?" he said.

NINE

Chateau And Cave

Twenty hours later, Reginald, Maurice, and Nikki were crammed into a shipping crate in the belly of a 747 bound for Paris, next to a kennel containing some kind of a hound dog that wouldn't stop barking. They were all going to be late for work on Monday — perhaps a few weeks late. None among the three called Berger to let him know that they would be away. The nice thing about being a vampire, Reginald thought, was that he could tell his boss that he was going to need some time off after the fact, and the boss would always cheerfully grant it.

They'd taken a red eye into New York. Once there, they'd taken a 4am cab to a nondescript industrial building, where Maurice had a friend and associate he'd called before they'd boarded their first flight. Maurice handed over a significant stack of cash, and the man (whose name was actually "Jimbo") beckoned them into a crate with a wave not unlike that of a five-star maitre d'. Jimbo then sealed the crate, and many hours later, they heard the beeping and whirring of a forklift and felt themselves moving.

Maurice apologized for the accommodations — especially to Nikki, who insisted on traveling with the vampires rather than topside in comfort — and told them that the flight back would be much more comfortable. He explained that taking a commercial eastbound transatlantic flight was a very, very bad idea for a vampire. Even if you left at 9pm while it was still dark, the flight lasted seven hours — and thanks to the time difference, would set you down in Paris at 9am. Except in the dead of winter, it was nearly impossible to fly eastward overseas in total darkness, and even then, you were taking a huge risk if there was a delay, or if you ended up sitting on the tarmac. It wouldn't matter if you closed your window, because most people kept them open. And then there was also the gap between the jetway and the plane, the windows in the airport, and any ground transportation to contend with.

On the return flight, they'd be able to leave at 10pm and arrive home at midnight. Time enough, even, to make a connection home without having to overnight in New York.

"Assuming we're still alive," said Maurice.

"Naturally," said Reginald.

Maurice laid back against the side of the crate and adjusted a small, battery-powered lantern.

"Ironically, even with paying Jimbo and bribing customs, going over in a crate doesn't cost much more than three last-minute plane tickets," said Maurice.

"Four," said Reginald. "I need two seats."

"And there's so much legroom!" said Nikki. Then she waved a small notebook overhead. "And look! I brought Mad Libs!"

Once they landed, there was more noise and more forklifting as the crate was moved again. Then a scratching noise came from the crate's edges, followed by the squealing of pulled nails. The side of the crate came open, and they found themselves in what looked like a hangar, blinking against bright warehouse lights.

"End of ze line, vamps," said a man in greasy overalls with a thick French accent. "I am supposed to tell you *not* to eat me. I am… how you say? 'On your side.'"

Maurice thanked the man, then tipped him like a skycap.

It was dark outside. There was a large digital clock on the wall of the warehouse that gave the time as 22:12, or 10:12pm. They walked through a small man door next to a giant rolling door large enough to accommodate an aircraft without wings, out into the Paris night.

"Smells French," said Reginald.

"Ironically, I just got back from Paris," said Nikki. "I should have stayed. So are you finally going to tell us where exactly we're going?"

Nikki had been antsy for the entire trip. Neither Reginald nor Maurice had wanted her to come on a dangerous, end-of-the-world vampire errand. She'd insisted, saying that she hadn't wanted to go on the *last* "dangerous vampire errand" either, but that she'd been a champ back then and hence should be allowed to decide for herself now. So to get back at her, neither Reginald nor Maurice would tell her their half of the joint reason for coming to France.

"I think I've figured out where Balestro will show up again in 26 days,'" said Reginald.

"Cradle of civilization? Nile Valley?" said Nikki.

"South Germany. A big hill, with a huge stone on the top."

"Famous place?"

"Not at all," said Reginald. "It's in a park. I think kids sled down it. Not this time of year, though."

"So how do you know that's where he'll be?"

"Because he said I'd know," said Reginald. He didn't tell her the rest, which was that he knew about the German sled hill because it had been in his mind ever since they'd met Balestro, as if Balestro had beamed it into his head. It was like Richard Dreyfus and Devil's Tower in *Close Encounters of the Third Kind*. He'd even caught himself carving the hill out of mashed potatoes one night at dinnertime.

Nikki turned to Maurice. "And *your* secret?"

"Luxembourg," said Maurice.

"What's Luxembourg?" said Reginald, who'd never been outside of the US.

"I thought you said we were going to France," said Nikki. "Why did you say we were going to France if we were actually going to Luxembourg?"

"What's Luxembourg?" repeated Reginald.

"This is why," Maurice told Nikki, cocking a thumb at Reginald. Then he turned to Reginald. "Luxembourg is a very small country wedged between France, Germany, and Belgium. Don't worry, you're hardly the only person who's never heard of it. Luxembourg's position puts it right in the middle of Western Europe and, because it ends up being neutral ground more or less by default, it's the perfect seat for the EU Vampire Council."

Maurice had already explained that even though the American Council acted as if it was the only game in town, it wasn't. There was an EU Council, a Far East Council, a South Pacific Council, a South American Council, and several others. America's Vampire Nation was the largest in population and had more or less cut off relations with the others, declaring itself independent and self-sufficient. There seemed to be more behind Maurice's statement about the American Nation's independence, but he didn't volunteer it. He only said that he'd come overseas years ago looking for a better life and had been torn ever since. Vampires had a far, far better network in America, but they also had what he called an "American edge."

"Before we leave Paris, do we at least get to show Reginald the Eiffel Tower, with its Eye of Sauron on the top?" said Nikki.

"I'm afraid not," said Maurice. "We've got a bit of a train ride yet."

They took a cab to the train station, then boarded a train from Paris to Metz Ville, where they transferred to a second train that took them on to Luxembourg City. Maurice apologized for the multiple rides and the length of the trip, explaining that he couldn't find a direct TGV that traveled late enough to not kill them. Reginald said he understood and supported Maurice's decision.

Reginald thought they were done once they reached Luxembourg City, but Maurice explained that their final destination was actually a small town in the south of the country called Differdange. Then he explained that they'd missed the last train to Differdange and would need to wait until 5am to catch the first train of the day, so they walked the city while Reginald fought to stay awake. Nikki, on the other hand, was as chipper as if she were on amphetamines.

"It's so cute!" she said, patting Reginald on the back. "Isn't it cute? I love Europe. I mean, Paris last week — last week, what the hell! — was my first time here, but I loved that, but the thing about Paris is... Hey, Reginald! Talking to you. The thing about Paris is that it's really not all that different from, like, New York, whereas this is, like, *quaint*, and..."

Reginald discovered that he could almost sleep while walking. The hours passed, and he found his mind wandering to a hill in Germany with a giant stone at the top… almost like an altar.

Several hours later, at precisely 5:05am, their quiet train rolled out of the Luxembourg station and they found themselves traveling past rolling countryside and isolated towns that Nikki said looked like they belonged on a Christmas card. Each time the train stopped, somnolent passengers embarked and disembarked, nobody speaking, many listening to headphones, most heads down, agreeing collectively not to break the spell of silence. To pass the time, Reginald watched foreign names pass the windows at each stop.

Berchem. Bettembourg. Noertzange.

Forty minutes later, at exactly 5:46, the train pulled onto an elevated platform above an old-world-looking town bearing a placard that read DIFFERDANGE. They stepped off, descended a flight of stairs, walked under the tracks, and emerged into a twilit world like none Reginald had ever seen before.

"Plenty of time to spare," said Maurice, looking at the eastern sky, which was beginning to lighten slightly.

"I don't like cutting it this close," said Nikki. "Can you imagine how embarrassing it would be for me if you two started burning to ash in the middle of a train? Worse than being caught with toilet paper stuck to my shoe."

Maurice just shook his head and laughed. "European trains, Nikki. You can literally set your watch by them. I told you it'd be fine."

As Maurice led them down the dark street, Reginald took it all in. The streets were narrow. The buildings looked old, but not run down. It would be more accurate to say they had an old *style*, perhaps, and were somehow foreign in a way Reginald couldn't place. The shapes of the road signs were different. The fonts used on the signs and buildings was different. There were very few people walking around, but those who were appeared… *different*. It was hard to pinpoint; maybe something to do with their clothing. All Reginald knew was that he felt very out of place, as if he stuck out like a sore thumb.

"Why is everything in French?" said Nikki.

"Not everything," said Reginald. He pointed up at a street sign that announced that they were on 'Rue J.F. Kennedy.'

"That's French" said Nikki.

"Not Kennedy," said Reginald. "*Er ist ein Berliner*, or so they say."

"They have three official languages here," said Maurice, speaking like a tour guide. "German, French, and a local dialect called Luxembourgish. You won't usually see Luxembourgish written. Pretty much everything is in French or German. Do either of you speak French or German?"

"No," said Nikki.

"Yes," said Reginald, who'd gotten bored one night and learned fifty languages because it seemed like a nice, round number.

"Most of the people speak English," he said. "Though I might try my French back on; I haven't gotten to use it in so long."

"Where is HQ?" said Nikki.

Maurice chuckled. "You'll see. This is so cool."

Reginald almost laughed himself just from watching Maurice. He was giddy. There was no other word for it.

They were passing a wide spot between two buildings. It seemed to be a parking lot or a wide driveway. Maurice pointed past the concrete, to a set of stone steps that climbed a hill to what could only be described as a castle.

"That's where we're going," he said.

"Looks like a castle," said Nikki.

"It *is* a castle," said Maurice. "But they call it a chateau. 'Chateau de Differdange.'"

"Those kids are going up there," said Nikki, nodding at a group of five people in their early twenties who had gotten off the train in front of them. They were quiet, as if the early hour had laid a spell over them. But they looked different in a different way — different enough to cancel out the negatives and return to Reginald's version of normal.

"They're Americans," said Reginald.

Maurice nodded. "The Chateau is a school now. It's actually a bona-fide campus of the University of Miami. That's the one in Ohio, not Florida. The Miami University Something-or-Other Center, or MUDEC for short, but the kids and staff just call it 'The Chateau.' Run by locals, with some American teachers on exchange, and attended by American college kids, mostly from MU of Ohio, who are somewhat obnoxious in their American way when they hit the local bars, but who are more or less good kids."

Reginald was looking at all those steps. "Do they have an elevator?" he said.

"Welcome to Europe," said Maurice, slapping Reginald good-naturedly on the back. "You'd lose weight here if you were capable of it."

"Maurice," said Nikki as they walked toward the stairs. "How do you know so much about this place?"

"I keep good ties with the EU Council and come here as a liaison now and again. This is its permanent home and has been since around the time Logan took over in America. It was built by a friend of mine, Wilhelm, back in the 1500s. Wilhelm built a castle on top of the hill and painstakingly had catacombs dug out beneath it to house those who chose to come and stay. At the beginning, it was more like a home for traveling vampires than anything having to do with government, so its heritage means that it's always felt more like a hostel."

"The European Council doesn't move around?" said Nikki.

Maurice shook his head. "They're not as paranoid as the Americans. Being Deacon of the American Council is like being the president. Being Deacon of the EU Council is like being a small town mayor or even a school headmaster — or, as I said, the fellow who runs a hostel. It's simply not something that vampires rip each other's throats out to take leadership of."

The stone steps were steep. Reginald hung tight to the railing and fought to keep his breath under control. The five kids ahead of them hadn't noticed them or didn't seem to care. Then all eight of them, in two groups, arrived at the top and made their way toward a door at the back of the castle.

"Wait… we're going *into the school?* With *humans*?"

"Yes. Wilhelm and his people, who always had a flair for the dramatic, moved to Transylvania of all places a while back and left the Chateau to a trust managed by the Council leadership. The Council was always short on money, so they began leasing out the residential portion of the Chateau, originally to vampire dignitaries. But when Miami University came knocking, the EU's current Deacon — a man named Karl Stromm, who you'll meet — realized that at least MUDEC would offer a key advantage over leasing to vampires. Specifically, they'd be invested in the building and wouldn't flit off every few months and require him to find new renters. So he figured why the hell not and did the deal."

They'd reached the back door. The group of students had already vanished inside, so Maurice typed a code on a keypad to open the door. They walked into a split level area and went down a short flight of steps. Reginald could hear the group of students moving around upstairs.

"Isn't it a bit early for school?" Nikki whispered.

"Yes. But it's more than a school, and kids hang out on and off for a lot of the day. We're right at the cutoff. Students mostly start showing up closer to seven and eight, and we're required to be inside by six, which is why we haven't seen any other vampires out here. Pretty much guaranteed, the five kids we just saw are the only kids here. They'll stay upstairs. Come on."

Maurice led them into a large finished basement with red brick walls that curved into a low overhead ceiling. Reginald found himself wanting to duck. It was like being in a giant underground wine cask. On one end was a TV and a set of couches and chairs.

"This is the Cave," said Maurice.

"Kav?"

"*Cave*," said Maurice, pronouncing it so it rhymed with *suave*. "But spelled C-A-V-E."

"Oh," said Reginald. "*Cave*." Pronouncing it so it rhymed with *Dave*.

"Yes. But don't say it so American-like, American," said Maurice, still giddy. Reginald found himself wondering why, if Maurice so clearly missed Europe, he'd stayed in America so long.

They crowded into a corner of the Cave opposite the TV, to the side of a set of doors. Maurice snaked a finger into a hole between two bricks, then did something to another set of bricks with his other hand. He pulled, and a door swung open. The seam at the door's edges was actually in the center of the mortar and had been totally invisible. The design was brilliant, and Reginald realized it had probably been done with tools no more sophisticated than trowels.

Once they were through the door and onto a landing at the top of a stone staircase, Maurice closed the door using a large handle that was mounted on the other side.

"This is the entrance to the catacombs," he said. "Vampire territory. Above is human territory. Now, there are a few rules here. First rule — and I'm sure you've already assumed this — is that all of the humans on Chateau grounds are totally and completely off-limits. No feeding, no glamouring. Do your best to have no contact whatsoever. See those monitors?" He motioned to a pair of video screens mounted next to the door. "Always check them before you leave the catacombs. This one sees the other end of the Cave, as if you were looking through a peephole in the door. This one shows around the corner, where the kids have a bank of lockers. If you see anyone on either of the screens, don't open the door.

"Second rule is that you can only come and go between 11pm and 6am. If it's 6:30am and it's winter and you've still got hours of darkness outside, you can't leave. You've got to wait until eleven. The school's human hours are more or less from seven or eight AM until around ten PM, so we stay down here during those times."

Something wasn't clicking for Reginald. He said, "But they know we're here?"

"Just the director. And I know what you're thinking, but you've got to understand that all of us were once human, and not all humans and vampires are bigots. To an enlightened few humans, we're no different from another minority race or people with a disability. Most white people wouldn't lease half of a duplex from blacks and then invade their half and kill them. It's the same with us and a few key people on the MUDEC board. We're their landlords, and we're in business together. It's been a long time since Europe was villagers with pitchforks and torches."

"Do they ever come down here?" Reginald asked.

Maurice chuckled. "Karl and his people are open-minded, but they're not stupid. Humans don't have anywhere near the finger strength required to open that door, it can't be forced with tools, and this entire section of wall is reinforced with steel. There are also several other exits from the catacombs that the humans know nothing about. It's safe enough, Reginald. Don't let the paranoia of the Americans sway you."

They rounded a corner, and the steps became a wide stone staircase that led them along a hewn rock wall, down into a large and echoey space. Further down, the chamber became highly ornate in an old-world craftsman sort of way. The walls were made of large bricks that looked like they had carefully been laid by hand. There were columns and pillars. The ceiling arched overhead like a giant cathedral, and every twenty feet or so along the wall was a torch in a sconce. The torches were the only source of light, giving the place a dramatic feel. Even the air felt different underground.

It occurred to Reginald that *this* was the kind of place vampires should gather, not topside in abandoned malls, inside of a light-sealed, mobile Council building made of steel and plastics.

A voice came from behind them.

"Maurice!"

They turned and Reginald saw a man in an ornate red robe walking briskly toward them. He and Maurice embraced, and then the newcomer stepped back with Maurice held at arm's length. He looked him over from head to toe and said, "You are looking well, my friend. It has been too long. It is good to see you again."

Maurice and the man in the red robe turned to face Reginald and Nikki.

"Reginald, Nikki," said Maurice. "Meet Karl Stromm, Deacon of the European Vampire Council."

TEN

Old World

Karl was everything Reginald expected a vampire to be before he'd become one.

He was dark, tall, and slim without being frail. His robe was very long and dragged behind him when he walked. He had a kind of inner radiance but wasn't classically handsome, and if Reginald had to guess at his human age, he'd estimate that Karl had been in his mid forties when he'd become a vampire. He had a gigantic nose, very dark eyebrows, and skin that looked weathered. His hair was long and black, tied back into a pony tail and bound with an ornate ring that looked as if it might be made of ivory. His teeth were crooked, and he had a large adornment in his right ear that looked like a massive fang or claw. Something white and sharp, anyway.

His bearing, despite what Maurice had said about the EU Council being like a small town government, was regal. It was something about the way he carried his head and used his body. Everything was dramatic. When he reached for anything, he rolled his wrist and flourished his palm before picking it up. When he entered a new room, he paused at the entrance, closed his eyes, inhaled, and rolled his neck slowly back in a semicircle. When he met Nikki, he'd taken her hand and kissed it. When he met men, he hugged them. His gestures were intimate and androgynous. And — this was interesting — Reginald thought he could smell powder on his skin.

Maurice made introductions around, but it was obvious that Karl already knew who they were and their entire backgrounds, including Reginald's rebellious vampire past and Nikki's humanity, which Karl promised "with a blood oath" would not cause her any problems while in his house. He didn't seem remotely surprised by Reginald's size, which Reginald found both strange and refreshing.

"So," said Karl, turning back to Maurice. "I hear the angels are giving you trouble."

Maurice looked like he'd been slapped.

"Is not true?" said Karl.

Reginald leaned closer to Maurice. "I guess you can stop worrying about how we're going to convince him."

"It's true," said Maurice. "I'm just… give me a minute."

Karl looked at Reginald and Nikki. "Maurice is jet lagged?"

"I've just never… you believe in angels?" said Maurice.

"Of course. I have met one a few times. He is annoying when in human form, but amuses me nonetheless."

"Karl…"

"You are still a skeptic? *Grüß Gott.* You have been in America too long. How many times have I told you about how I talk to angels?"

"I thought you were being figurative. Like how my crazy neighbor talks to angels."

"Well," Karl said to Reginald, slapping Maurice on the shoulder. "Now he knows, am I right? Come."

Karl turned, made an extravagant little gesture with his hand, and pulled a torch from a sconce. He led them to the other end of the chamber and through a smaller stone archway.

"We are light this morning," he said without turning. "I am sorry. Most here keep a traditional schedule and are already beginning for the sleep. This chamber we are coming to, you will see. It fills up when everyone is awake. You've seen *The Matrix*? The second one, where they have that big party and all are almost having sex? Is like that, but take out the 'almost' and add biting." He laughed. "Is fun. You are exclusive?" He tossed a look at Maurice and Nikki.

Nikki was closer to Karl than Reginald. Unsure of how to answer the question, she simply nodded.

"Shame. I would like to have sex with both of you. You change your mind and decide to do the orgy, you let me know and I will be there." He said it like it was an offer to loan them a belt sander.

They passed several corridors and chambers, and Karl pointed to each like a tour guide. He indicated residence areas, baths and showers, and even a kitchenette.

"Usually just coffee and cigarettes, which many of us still enjoy. But Maurice, he is a true friend to you," said Karl, looking at Reginald. "So after he tells us how you like to eat and that you are bringing a human, we have gotten some special things to welcome you. You will see later. I will spoil one, is donuts. You know donuts? They are strange to me. They are round, but with a hole like a tire." He turned and made a circle with his hands so that they'd understand.

Reginald hoped they'd gotten more than just sweets. He was fine with junk food, but Nikki was normally a very healthy eater. He didn't trust vampires to understand nutrition, as well-intentioned as they may be. It was like a set of lame parents trying to pick out cool clothing for their teenager. It just wasn't something they knew much about.

They came to an intimate chamber with brick walls and another low ceiling. In the center was a large wooden conference table, and Reginald found himself remembering Logan's old wooden throne. Apparently that bit of paranoia hadn't made it overseas yet, either. But then, the walls were also lined with wooden torches, and he'd seen many wooden supports and beams. The crossbeam architecture in some of the places they'd passed reminded him of pictures he'd seen of Switzerland. It felt a bit like being deep beneath an elaborate gingerbread house.

As they entered the room, Reginald realized there were other vampires already present. All were dressed similarly to Karl. Two of the men had large white hairdos that Reginald suspected were powdered wigs. The men were holding hands. All of the women were either wearing corsets or simply had tiny waists and huge breasts with massive cleavage that came up to their chins. Reginald counted the vampires already present in the room. There were twelve of them.

"Here is our Council room. And here is the Council members." He named them all, then named Nikki, Maurice, and Reginald. Every member of the Council embraced each of the newcomers. The men kissed Nikki's hand, as Karl had. Too late, Reginald wondered if he was expected to kiss the female Council members' hands. He had one left to meet, so he took her hand and raised it while lowering his head. Her chest got in the way, and his face planted firmly in her cleavage. He looked up, embarrassed, but the woman giggled and grabbed his crotch. Next to him, Nikki reddened, but Reginald told her with his eyes to let it go. Nikki greeted the woman cordially, but then grabbed Reginald's crotch herself to make it clear who it belonged to. Across from them, the two men in powdered wigs grabbed each other's crotches and one of the women put her face into the cleavage of one of the other women.

"So," said Karl, motioning to the table, "tell us about your angel issue."

Reginald watched the others. Nobody reacted.

"I'm sorry," said Reginald. "Just to get this out there, do I take it that you all believe the story of the Six founding fallen angels?"

The vampires around the table looked at each other as if unsure how to answer the question.

"They do," said Karl. "They hesitate because the question is strange to us. It's like you asked if I believe in... in Maurice." He put a hand on Maurice's shoulder.

"Did you know this about them?" Reginald asked Maurice.

"I understand why you are surprised," Karl said to Reginald. "Maurice was always a skeptic. I have always known, of course, but Maurice has not met one in person yet."

"But you have?"

"Sure."

Maurice put his head on the table.

"Go ahead and tell us your story, Maurice" said Karl.

Maurice looked up and, after a moment, began speaking. He told the Council about the two incidents at the American Council meetings and about Reginald's deductions. The deductions involving the existence of angels didn't, of course, surprise anyone at the table, but they became more interested when he explained what he thought of Balestro's ominous declaration, the waiting period, and the difficulty (and likely futility) of redemption.

"So," said a man with brown hair and a prominent mole on his forehead, "you think they mean to end all of us?"

"I think it's very possible," said Reginald.

"All of us, or just the Americans?" said Karl. "Because he goes to you, not us. This is the first we are hearing."

"Not to be pigheaded," said Reginald, "but does it matter?"

"Yes," said Karl. "Is okay with me if they kill the American Council."

Several of the others made noises of protest.

"What?" said Karl. "American vampires are *sheisse*. I am just saying what we are all thinking, right?"

"Karl," said Maurice, "*we* are American vampires. I know there's been a bit of a schism in relations and thinking, but it wouldn't just be the Council; it'd surely be all of us. You can't be condoning genocide."

"*Fine*," said Karl, sighing. "American vampires are A-number-one."

"Besides," said Reginald, "I don't think it's just the American Vampire Nation's problem. The place where Balestro will return in —"

"About three weeks," said Nikki.

"— in three weeks is just outside of Holzkirchen. A hill, with a giant stone at the top, like an altar…"

"I know the place," said Karl. "I'm from München. Is a place of some note in the past, but it is now just a sled hill."

"So if he's going to come back there, and that's in Europe…"

"Then why were we not told?"

"There's no way this won't sound self-centered," said Reginald, "but it seemed like he was coming to *me*. It seemed like he was telling *me*. It wasn't about the American

Council versus the other Councils. It was about me instead of anyone else."

"Why you?" said the man with the brown hair.

"I have no idea."

"So," said Karl. "To 'right the game,' as you say, Maurice, we do what?"

"I really don't know. What would make you want to keep playing a game of chess after you were nearly checkmated?"

Karl nodded toward a beautiful woman across the table. "If Lola takes her top off during a chess game, I will stay interested."

"If you could somehow get pieces back," said Reginald, ignoring Karl's joke. "If your opponent lost some of his pieces. If the rules of the game changed so that you were no longer at a disadvantage."

"How can we do any of that?" said Lola. "Turn people? Kill people?" She sighed. "I'm over three thousand years old. I'll be honest; I've lost my taste for both."

There was a loud sound. Reginald looked over to see that Karl had slapped the table with the palm of his hand.

"So!" he said. "We could keep guessing, but why? Let's ask."

"Ask who?" said Maurice.

"Santos."

"Who is Santos?"

"*Engel*," said Karl.

"Wait… you know where to *find* one of the Six?"

"Of course," said Karl. "He is usually in town. When he is not, we wait and he always returns."

Maurice squinted and shook his head. Then Lola cleared her throat.

"We, um… used to date," she said. Then a shiver ran through her and she added, "I don't like to talk about it."

ELEVEN

Scheisskopf

Santos the angel was maybe five-foot-four, pudgy, and smelled bad.

It took ten days to find him. Karl, Maurice, Nikki, Reginald, and Lola headed out the day after their first meeting and came up empty. They tried the following day and the day after with the same result. Each time they failed, Karl threw up his hands and said good-naturedly, "So, he is not back yet. We should orgy?" Reginald, Nikki, and Maurice declined, but it was getting harder and harder to refuse. Karl made it sound like an invitation to imbibe the local culture, and turning him down was beginning to feel dismissive of his hospitality.

On their tenth day in Differdange, they found Santos exactly where Karl said he always eventually showed up: at a local bar called *Getränkspeil*, passed out in a booth in the corner. He was wearing a shirt that was too tight, stained, and ripped, and he had at least three days' worth of beard growth on his face. He'd slumped sideways, his face against the side wall of the booth, his lip pulled up to expose a row of black teeth. His beer mug was on the floor, intact but sideways. Beer on the floor mingled with what appeared to be vomit. He was snoring loudly.

Lola had explained that a very long time ago, she'd lived in Egypt as a slave. The pharaoh ("one of the Ramesseses, I forget which, it was a long time ago," she said) had called in a group of female slaves, and the pharaoh had been particularly taken with her above the others. That was how she first met the man who today called himself Santos.

"You hear how the pharaohs were worshipped, like god-kings?" she said. "Well, most were just men, but this one was actually a god. He only ruled a while, then got bored. He wanted a consort, and I was flattered and glad to no longer be a slave. He liked me. He made me a vampire so I would not become old. Then, after a few hundred years, I got tired of him and left him. He's been obsessed with me since."

"Angels get obsessed?" said Nikki.

Lola nodded. "They become like humans in order to exist here on Earth. But when they are like humans, they are subject to human emotions, needs, and desires. Santos has spent so much time pining that he is almost handicapped. He is in human form most of the time, and to me he is a constant pest. He cannot force me to love him because of free will, so he becomes depressed and he drinks."

Still, despite Lola's explanation, Reginald wasn't expecting the pathetic form they found. He'd expected a tortured man who was still radiant and elegant-looking, but what they found was gross and ugly and smelled like he'd soiled himself.

"Santos," said Lola.

The unconscious form didn't move. Lola shoved him with her foot.

"Santos," she repeated.

The form grumbled, so this time she actually kicked him. When he yelped, she explained, "They can feel pain when they are like this, too." Then she wrinkled her nose and said, "Just a big sack of meat."

"What?" said the ugly man.

"Santos. It's me. Lola."

"Isis?"

"I'm Lola now," she said. Then she turned to the others and said, "Not *that* Isis. It used to be a popular name."

"Mmm," said the form in the booth.

"Santos. Get up, you drunken shit." She nudged him again.

"Lemme be."

Nikki turned to Karl. "Are you sure that *this*... person... is a... you know...a...?"

"Nicole Jane Pilsen," said Santos, straightening up. "Graduated high school 2001, 4th in your class, lost your virginity in a Mazda Miata behind a Taco Bell. When it was over, your exact words were, 'Well, that was interesting.' Afterward you went bowling with the guy, and when you noticed that he had a giant cum stain on the front of his pants, you ran out the back door and hitched a ride home with a man named Telly."

"... an angel," Nikki concluded.

"I must apologize for his appearance," said Lola. "I don't want you thinking I would be with... *this*. Angels can take human form, but the form they take is like their mood. When he is sad, he looks sad, and when he is sad, he gets drunk and it gets worse." She kicked Santos yet again and Reginald felt himself flinch, unable to believe she was treating what was essentially her literal creator so harshly.

Lola shook her head, disgusted. "The last time I saw him and he was not like this form, he was the Unabomber."

"He looked like the Unabomber?" said Reginald.

"He *was* the Unabomber," Lola repeated.

"I got bored," said Santos, who seemed compelled to explain himself.

"Purge yourself," said Lola.

"No."

"*Santos.*"

"No."

She leaned forward and whispered something to him.

"Fine," he said. The man in the booth vanished in a flash of blue light. An instant later, there was another flash and a new man appeared in his place. The new man was tall, with fine strawberry blonde hair and a square chin.

"We shall be just a moment," said the new Santos, rising from the booth. He took Lola's hand. She shook it off, then began walking toward a back hallway. Santos followed.

"Charmed to meet you," he said as he walked off.

It was five minutes before Santos and Lola returned from what appeared to be the women's bathroom. While they waited, Karl explained that all it took for an angel to shake off whatever mortal baggage he or she had accumulated during a stint as a human was to reemerge into a non-corporeal form and then become a human again. Karl likened the process to a dirty person jumping into a lake and emerging clean. He said that Lola had almost certainly bribed him to do it by promising him a quickie in the bathroom.

"He will now follow her around for months," said Karl. "This will only encourage him." He added that if Santos would simply spend more time in his natural form instead of being constantly in flesh on the mortal plane, he'd lose all of his interest in Lola because angels were, in and of themselves, emotionless and dispassionate. But he said that what Santos had was an addiction — and that just like with any addiction, the more he indulged in it, the worse the addiction became.

When the pair returned, Santos seemed refreshed and Lola seemed disgusted. She excused herself and left the bar, presumably to return to the Chateau for a shower.

The tall man that Santos had become sat across from Reginald and smiled.

"So you're him," said the angel. His voice contained no accent. It was crisp and clean and perfect.

"Excuse me?" said Reginald.

"You're the one Balestro came to. Interesting choice. I see why. I owe a favor to Isis. Lola. How may I help you, Reginald?"

"So you're in this with Balestro?"

"Yes and no. Think of us less like six individuals and more like six heads of one being. What one does, we all do. We neither agree nor disagree. We simply do and are."

"So you're in constant communication with him? Like now?"

"Not when mortal. We all flit in and out of mortal. We reconnect when we return to our non-corporeal states. It's not unlike plugging one device into another periodically to sync them."

"So by talking to you, it's like I'm talking to him?"

"You are talking to me. When I reemerge into a non-corporeal form, it will be as if you've talked to him."

Reginald shook his head. "It's all very confusing."

And so the angel smiled and said, "Would you like me to show you?"

TWELVE

Evolved

The place Reginald suddenly found himself wasn't white. It wasn't black. It was nothing at all. He couldn't see, but he wasn't blind. He couldn't hear, but he wasn't deaf. He was somehow a disembodied intelligence. He wasn't floating, but he wasn't grounded, either. It was like being weightless in a realm where the idea of weight had no meaning. He tried to blink, but he didn't have eyelids. He didn't have anything. The feeling was like waking from anesthesia. He had no idea how he'd gotten here — wherever "here" was — and could only take it in as it presented itself, hoping that it would all soon make sense.

"We call this the anteroom," said a voice. It was Santos's voice, but Reginald suddenly felt quite sure that he was only hearing Santos's voice because it's what he expected to hear. And then, because he'd had that thought, the next voice he heard was less of an actual voice and more of a feeling, as if it were coming directly into his mind.

"You are not supposed to be here. You cannot stay long. Ask your question. Be quick."

The voice was dry and devoid of inflection, totally unlike the newer Santos's polite voice in the bar. It was as if he were talking to someone else. But of course, if this "anteroom" was what he thought it was, then he *was* talking to someone else. In a way, he was talking to all six of them.

"The others," said Reginald. "Are they here?"

"The question has no meaning. We are. I am. You are."

"Is Balestro here?"

"The question is senseless. Yes. In a way that is sufficiently true in your capacity to understand, he is here."

"Am I speaking to him now?"

"Irrelevant. No. But also yes."

"Are you planning to destroy the race of vampires?"

"Yes."

"Will you succeed?"

"Of course. We are immortal and omnipotent. You think you are immortal, but you are not. You can be killed. It is simple to do so."

Reginald's spirit, or whatever it was, floated in the voidless void. The sensation was hard to put a finger on.

Eventually, Reginald said, "Why are you going to do it?"

"Do what?"

"Destroy the vampires."

There was a pause. Reginald wondered if maybe an answer wasn't coming. Then the voice said, "Because your kind is a failure."

"Because the humans outnumber us?"

"What is a number?"

Reginald waited for more, but there was no more.

"I don't understand," said Reginald.

"Correct. You do not," said the voice.

Reginald floated and waited. The silence was complete. There was no white noise, no nothing at all.

"This would be easier if you'd stop being so obtuse," said Reginald.

"This would be easier if you'd ask for what you wanted," said the voice.

"Did you make a bet? With the one humans call God?"

"No. Your myths are not true, but they are true enough. It is hard to convey. So yes. In a way that is sufficiently true by your capacity to understand, yes. There was a wager. A bet."

"And was it like a game? A bet over a game?"

"In a way that is sufficiently true by your capacity to understand, yes."

Reginald couldn't help but feel that the voice was insulting him.

"By the rules of your game, what did vampires do to lose?"

"At the beginning of time, which is to say the beginning of human time, of vampire time, we split the pure nature that was ourselves into two halves. One was given the day. The other was given the night. One was given the tools of the predator. One was given the defenses and the instincts of prey. One was given aggression. One was given protection. One could live forever but had certain mortal weaknesses. The other was much weaker and mortal, but was stronger in terms of will and ambition. Two halves, two brothers, two created from the same source. The light and dark natures of the source were split into a perfect good and a perfect evil. But there was a flaw inherent to the nature of the schism. Both natures became polluted. Humans imbibed evil. Vampires, some of them, imbibed good. Humans became possessed of an evil nature which they had to fight to subdue, and which most of them successfully subdued. You embraced your evil nature and did not embrace the good. You magnified your singular nature. Gloried in it. Your compassion did not grow to consume you, to war within you, as evil did within humans. Humans became whole. You remained half. Humans learned to rule the day and the night, learned to master good and evil. You gloried in your curse and ruled only the night and the darkness. What you were, you sought to become more of. You were strong, so you became stronger. You were fast, so you became faster. You were long-living, so you sought immortality. You fed, so you wanted to feed more. Never did you evolve. Never did you change in any way that was not already within your nature. And when the curse was magnified, when your evolution became slower and slower and stopped, you didn't fight it. You embraced it. You turned your back on anything that wasn't within your experience. You purged what had polluted you. And as you did, the game began to end. Our challenger had once boasted to us, 'Give me a seed of purity, and it will grow even amongst pollution so long as the soil is sound.' We replied, 'Will is weak, and any strong seed will grow in any soil.' We were wrong. Humans became more. You became less. Through their strength, humans have learned to cope with what threatens them, with enemies both great and small. All that's left before you die by their hand is for them to realize you exist. Then your existence as parasites will end because you have remained of a nature that is singular and incapable of adaptation."

Reginald waited until he was sure that the voice had finished. When he was sure, he said, "So let us fight. Now that we know, let us fight."

"The fight is lost. A good player knows when to surrender."

"Give us time."

"You have fifteen days."

"We can't evolve in fifteen days," said Reginald.

"True," said the voice.

"And?"

"And so, to borrow an expression from your language," said the voice, "You're fucked."

Reginald started to say something else, but then the floating sensation and the whiteness that wasn't white and the blackness that wasn't black was gone, and he found himself slumped in a booth in a bar in Differdange with the three others, and Santos was gone.

THIRTEEN

Turn

Reginald and Nikki lay on a bed in their room deep in the catacombs beneath the Chateau. Maurice was in the chamber next door and seemed to have gone to sleep. Nikki was asleep. Only Reginald lie awake, his mind for once struggling to assimilate and solve what he had experienced.

You have refused to evolve.

Interestingly, Reginald *had* evolved. Or at least, he felt that he represented a kind of evolution within the species. Maurice once said he'd never seen someone so physically ungifted and so correspondingly mentally gifted as Reginald. He couldn't help but feel that he, as the Vampire Nation's "step in the wrong direction," might actually be a step in the *right* direction — especially after what the voice in the void had said. Perhaps that was why Balestro had spoken to Reginald out of all of the vampires. Any geneticist could explain that when a population reached an evolutionary bottleneck, that population began to die. "Mistakes" like Reginald threatened to break the bottleneck because they were nothing if not diverse. And how much newness — how much diversity — had entered the vampire gene pool in the past few centuries? Vampires had gotten bigger, better, stronger, faster, and more beautiful. They'd refined as a species, just like how dog breeders carefully refined a breed of dogs... causing weaknesses inherent to inbreeding. What looked like improvement to the Council was actually stagnation, especially in the eyes of those that moved the chess pieces on the giant board.

Humans had grown, expanded, and conquered the night. Humans had been born as halflings, but had recaptured the wholeness they'd been born from. Night and day. Good and evil. Temperance and greed and up and down and...

He awoke hours later, not remembering having fallen asleep. Nikki was still asleep beside him. It was just after six PM. He had all the time in the world.

Except that he really only had two weeks. They all did.

"Maybe they'd let us — just the two of *us* — live," Maurice had said, walking with Reginald and Nikki back to the Chateau just before sunrise. "I'm old. I'm certainly more open to 'eliminating bottlenecking' than the entirety of the American Council, which is of course why they hate me. You were an accident, and the things you can do with your mind and your nervous system are definitely steps forward. Figure out how to breech the daytime and we'll be golden."

"Do you think it's that literal?" said Reginald. "What if we *could* walk during the daylight? Humans can't actually see in the dark. What they did was to adapt. They said, 'We can't do this one thing, so we'll change the rules of the game.' They didn't find ways to see in the dark, most of them. They found ways to *change the world* so that it wasn't dark."

"We're supposed to learn to manufacture darkness?"

"I don't know." He felt very tired, for once unable or possibly just uninterested in running through the permutations, the levels of meanings in what the angel had said. "I don't know, Maurice. I just want to sleep."

"Fifteen days. *Fifteen days.* Do you think you can evolve by then? Should we fly back and try to convince the American Council to come with us to meet Balestro on this hill of yours? Should we begin work on vampire-advancing innovations? Should we start worldwide psychoanalysis groups? Embark on mass turnings to increase our diversity? How about vampire libraries and symphonies? We could turn Tony Robbins and get his take on the whole self-improvement angle. Think that would do it?"

Reginald chuckled.

Maurice sighed. He looked into the east, where the bright smear on the sky above the horizon was growing marginally brighter.

"Suppose I just kept walking," he said. "Instead of turning up to the Chateau, suppose I walked too far. I could get a coffee down the street when the Starbucks opens, just to see if I've started to like it as you do. It's up there, around the corner; I saw it earlier. Maybe I could buy one of those sugary coffee drinks you always get, and just walk. Walk past the town, into the countryside, onto a deserted section of road, open to the sun when it rises. At my age, I wouldn't last long. There would probably be hardly any pain, and then it would all be over."

"Don't talk that way," said Nikki.

"Yeah, you're a lot older than me," said Reginald. "You're supposed to be my rock."

"I just can't help but wonder. If angels are real, is Heaven? Is Hell? And if we're the children of six fallen angels, where does that mean we are going?"

Reginald, who wasn't remotely religious even after recent events, shook his head.

"Did I ever tell you about how a few years ago, a group of vampire scientists were talking about partnering with people in NASA to launch a low orbit, geosynchronous craft, kind of like a space station? It would circle the earth once every 24 hours, moving west, always on the opposite side of the planet from the sun. They wanted to build a city. *That* would be evolution. Vampires in space instead of Pigs in Space. I don't suppose you have a line on some sort of a *Battlestar Galactica* plan to leave the planet, heading out in the path of the Earth's shadow, heading into deep space beyond the reach of the sun and the stars?"

Before Reginald or Nikki could say anything, Maurice smirked to himself.

"You live this long, you see this much, you'd think nothing could surprise you," he said.

Now, hours later in the quiet catacombs, Reginald thought back on Maurice's demeanor. The coldness of it bothered him, especially given how giddy Maurice had been just a day ago.

Feeling guilty, he rolled over and woke Nikki. He needed someone to talk to.

"He's had two thousand years to learn to cope" said Nikki after shaking off the cobwebs of sleep. "He'll be fine."

"Will he?"

"We all will," she said.

She sighed. Then, seemingly out of the blue, she said, "I was thinking earlier. I know how you must've felt, all those months ago."

"What do you mean, 'you know how I must've felt'?" said Reginald.

"I mean that I've finally been cleared by the American

Council to be turned into a vampire. It's something I've wanted and trained for years, and fought for, and studied for, and striven for. And now, if I were turned, I'd have just two weeks to be what I've always wanted to be."

"That's not how I felt at all," said Reginald.

"I mean that I've worked and worked, and I was ready to spend an eternity being my own vision of perfect. But if these 'angels' or whatever they are…"

"You're perfect right now," said Reginald.

She smiled a small, artificial smile and put a hand to his cheek. "That's sweet. But it's also bullshit."

Reginald had brought some of the snack foods in from the kitchenette. As he'd suspected, almost all of it turned out to be garbage. He pulled out a red tube of crackers with chocolate sandwiched between them that had looked interesting. The package proclaimed: *HIT*.

"I don't know, Reginald. This is something I've warred with, and fought with myself about, and gone back and forth on, and had finally, just recently, decided that I wouldn't ever have to face. I'm not ready for it."

"Angels?"

"Death. The existential horror of it all." She sat on the bed beside Reginald and looked him in the eyes.

Reginald unwrapped the *HIT* crackers and ate one. It was delicious. He waited for Nikki to go on, intuiting that it was still her turn.

"Did it ever seem strange to you," she said, "how easily I agreed to take such a big risk for you back at your trial all those months ago?"

Reginald looked back at Nikki, genuinely curious.

"You did it for Claire."

"Claire is a great girl," said Nikki. "And yes, I wanted to help her. But Reginald, you have to understand how that plan looked from where I was sitting. I know you had no doubts, and knowing you as I do now, I probably wouldn't have any doubts if you proposed it today. But I'd known you for a week at the time. *A week.* I'd known Claire for just a few days. What you told me seemed crazy. It felt like a million-to-one shot. There was no way I thought it'd work. Too much could go wrong. In your plan, I was supposed to be a vampire. But when the Guard came, I was sure they'd see that I didn't fight like a vampire. I was sure that when I 'extended my fangs,' the Guard would realize that they were costume shop knockoffs filled with incendiary powders. How could they not tell the difference?"

"They saw…"

"Yes, I know. They saw what they wanted to see. They were the wolves and I was the sheep, and nobody suspects the sheep. But I didn't know you well enough to trust your ability to read human and vampire nature back then. When we made it out alive, I thought it was sheer luck. And sometimes, even today, I still wonder if it *was* luck, because if you could really read people, you'd be able to read me. And you can't. I know you can't."

Reginald simply watched her, letting her say what she seemed to need to say.

"From where I was sitting, going to your trial was a one-way errand. I pretend to be a vampire. They haul me in. They kill you, and they kill Maurice. Then they see me still standing in the sunlight, and they kill me. But they don't just kill me. I've made them look like fools. So they rape me. They torture me. They drain me. And then, mercifully, it's all over."

Reginald set the crackers aside and put his hand on Nikki's leg. He felt oddly conflicted and oddly human. He'd known with very high certainty that Nikki would be safe, but he hadn't realized how sure she'd been that she would die. It changed the nature of both his request and her decision to accommodate it. He felt guilty, despite the outcome.

"If you were sure it was a dead end, why did you do it?" he said.

A single tear was making its way down the crease between her nose and her right cheek. She didn't seem to have noticed it.

"Because I wanted to die," she said.

Reginald didn't trust himself to say anything. He simply waited, and the wait felt very long.

"My parents died when I was young. They were both unbalanced, both on depression meds. We were constantly under financial pressure, because my dad made some very bad investments, then gambled away what was left. My mom hung in there for as long as she could, but it was always a losing battle. I used to wake up in the middle of the night to use the bathroom and see a light on downstairs. I always woke Jackie and she never complained, because we both knew that when Mom and Dad were awake in the middle of the night, it was because they were worried, and because neither was strong. So they'd just hold each other and cry. Can you imagine what it's like for kids to witness their parents so helpless, when parents are supposed to be the protectors?"

"How old were you?" said Reginald.

"Junior high," she said. "Jackie must've been in high school, like in the later years, because I remember that on the night our parents split a bottle of Seconal, after we called 911, she drove out to get us ice cream after it was all over. *Ice cream.* It sounds so ridiculous now, but we were grasping at straws. Anything to feel normal. To make it all go away for a few minutes or seconds."

Reginald didn't know what to say. Nikki had been shamelessly ebullient for pretty much the entirety of the time they'd known each other. He'd never known her to have dark moods, and she'd always seemed so forward and so incredibly open. But this was something she'd been protecting. And she was right. He'd never been able to read her at all.

"I told you that I found Maurice, and that he was my mentor," she said, wiping away the tear. "That's true. But what I didn't tell you was *when* and *how* I found him. I was seventeen. I was living with my grandmother, and I'd dropped out of school. I hung with a different kind of crowd. Not bad kids, but… outsiders. They made me laugh, but they also smoked and drank a ton. Maurice knew them somehow. I figured he was one of us. He became like a brother to me. We were never… together, though I wanted to be. Years later, when I realized how young I must have seemed to him, I understood. By then, I'd realized what he was. I begged him to turn me. I remember how shameless I was. I *begged*. I was angry. I wanted revenge. It didn't matter who I took that revenge out on. I wanted to feel in control. Any kind of power at all. But Maurice wouldn't do it. He didn't tell me to train — later, the official authorities did that — but he told me that I needed to be emotionally ready. That's the one part of all of this that he still believes in. It's all very Zen. 'Clear your mind and your soul before you decide what to commit your mind and soul to,' or something. He said there were right and wrong reasons to want to turn, and at the time, my reason was the wrong one. I hated him for that for a long time, but then, little by little, it got better and I came to thank him for making me wait. And the rest, you already know."

Reginald took a breath in, then let it out. Now his hand was on her cheek, and she smiled. He took it away.

"So you did it for Maurice," said Reginald.

"I did it because I never forgave myself," she said. "Becoming a vampire, it's like dying. And dying? Well, that's even closer. I don't remember consciously weighing the decision to do what you said. I just remember thinking that I could do it and die, or I could refuse and become a vampire and have that power and control I'd always wanted. I knew I was making the wrong choice, but I made it anyway. Looking back, that was my last truly dark moment. I think I'd decided that I'd finally found someone I could take revenge on: myself."

"I had no idea," he said.

She pursed her lips together into a thin line and looked at him, then shrugged.

Reginald couldn't read her as a vampire, but there was still plenty of human in him. He got up, sat across from her, and took both of her hands in his.

"Do you still want to die?" he said.

She shook her head, sniffed, and met his eyes. "Not in the same way I used to. A lot of that is thanks to you."

"You understand that whatever Balestro is or who he represents, they may just have a grudge against vampires. You understand that as a human, you'll probably be safe."

"*You'd*," she said. "You mean that I *would* be safe as a human, not I *will* be safe as a human." And softly, gently, her small hands squeezed his big ones. She leaned her head to the side. Her neck was long and smooth. Reginald could see her pulse. A strange hot feeling surrounded him like a cloud. He leaned closer.

"This is you punishing yourself," he said. But it was hard to speak.

"No. It's not."

"You'll turn. Then you'll die two weeks from now with the rest of us. You are choosing death over life."

"Not for certain."

"But likely. At least wait and see what happens."

"I believe in you," she said.

He shouldn't do it.

"I can't do it," he said.

"You have to. I've been thinking about it ever since Balestro, since getting my approval in the mail. It's not the wrong choice this time. *And it's mine to make.*"

Her neck was very close. He could feel the heat coming off of her skin.

"You're sure."

"Yes." It was almost a whisper.

"And you're sure you want it to be me. You want that bond."

His nostrils flared. His fangs extended.

"Yes."

Reginald closed his eyes and leaned in the rest of the way. His senses filled with the scent of her, of her flesh, of her body, of her blood.

And then the long wait, in both ways, slowly and slowly and slowly ended.

FOURTEEN

Dear Old Dad

Nikki announced her news to Maurice the next day by repeatedly running into his room and placing *HIT* crackers onto the dresser in his room when he wasn't looking. Eventually, after the fourth cracker appeared, Maurice noticed the odd brown-and-black discs and looked around. Nikki appeared in the doorway and said, "Oh, I'm sorry." And then, in a blur, she ran forward, removed the cracker sandwiches, ran back, and began eating one of them. She bounced the remaining crackers on her palm and smiled, and Maurice ran forward like a family greeting family at a big wedding, and wished her congratulations.

It didn't last long. Almost immediately after the hug, Maurice realized what this would mean for her as Reginald had, and began chastising her. Then he stormed in on Reginald, who was lying awake in bed, and began chastising *him*. The debate went on for two or three minutes. It ended when Nikki began quoting Maurice back to himself about heart and soul and mind and Zen, and then pointed out the simple fact that what was done was done, and that it had been her own damn choice.

Maurice relented, fatalistic, and the evening fell into what was beginning to feel like an old rhythm in a new place.

There was such a huge difference between the dawn of Nikki's vampire abilities and Reginald's that he felt a strange pang of jealousy. Where he'd been slow, she was lightning fast. Where he'd been weak, she was astonishingly strong. Nikki ran through the catacombs picking up everything large that wasn't nailed down. She kept picking up rocks and crushing them. When it was time to eat (the kitchenette had pouches of human blood that Reginald impaled with a straw like a Capri Sun), Nikki said she'd join him after she showered. Reginald began walking. When he arrived at the kitchenette thirty seconds later, Nikki was waiting for him in a chair, two blood pouches on the table, her hair clean and wet.

"Give her time," said Maurice later, sitting across from Reginald in Reginald and Nikki's room while Nikki was off exploring the catacombs. "It's always like this on the first night, when a new vampire's abilities captivate them."

"Not always," said Reginald.

"Hey, I remember you shamelessly doing a pushup," said Maurice.

Reginald told Maurice to get the fuck out of his room. Maurice told Reginald to make him. Then Nikki arrived in a blur and Reginald found himself flat on his back on the bed, his arms pinned above his head. Then she let him sit back up and made herself comfortable beside him.

"Thank you for my gift," she said, kissing him on the cheek. Then she noticed that she'd placed her hand on his crotch and pulled it back. It was the third time her hand had ended up in his crotch without her conscious awareness.

"Again, I'm sorry," she said, standing up and starting to

pace around the room. "It just keeps going there. Did this happen to you?"

"What?"

"The pervasive sexuality. Everything is making me horny. I was having some habit hunger earlier, so I went into the kitchenette and microwaved a hot dog. That was a mistake. I had to run into the bathroom after I ate it and take care of business. Oh, and just FYI, there are no more Fudgesicles in the freezer. I couldn't take it. I pitched all of them."

She paused.

"But then I couldn't stand the thought that they were still just sitting there in the garbage, so I pulled them out and melted them down under a stream of hot tap water."

"Wait," said Reginald. "Am I to understand that you've removed all of the Fudgesicles?"

"Twinkies too. And rocket pops. Strangely, the donuts aren't bothering me. I guess I don't swing that way."

"Among new vampire women, it's about fifty-fifty," said Maurice.

"So did this happen to you, Reginald?" she said.

"No. I became very interested in pizza."

"Weren't you already interested in pizza?"

Reginald took a bite of one of the non-offensive donuts he'd snagged earlier. "It ratcheted up a notch."

Despite her new vampire pallor, Nikki managed to flush. "Oh, Jesus. I just thought about that hot dog again. Is it always like this?"

Maurice shrugged. "You've still got a ton of human blood. Feeding and sex go together. Give it a week. After you're more vampire, it'll be more manageable. Especially after you lose your taste for human food."

"Ath if that vud haffen," said Reginald around a huge mouthful of donut.

"Oh Jesus. Oh Jesus." She was flitting around like a ball in a pinball machine. "It's *my human blood* that's doing this? I'm turning *myself* on?" She crossed her legs. "Hang on." There was a blur and she was gone. A door banged. She returned with a major tuft of hair sticking up on her head.

"I'm sorry, dear," she said, touching Reginald's arm. "I'm afraid that if this really is the end of our world, you're in for an ending filled with workouts."

Reginald raised the donut as if he were making a toast. "Fine by me. I'd better carb up." Then he took a bite.

A week passed, and neither Nikki's food hunger nor her sexual hunger abated. All she wanted to do was eat and have sex. Reginald wanted to see the sights, so in the evenings, they took what trains there were to the sites they could reach in the time they had and looked at ruins and attractions. Nikki kept stopping for crepes and pastries and to pull Reginald into bathrooms and hidden areas in parks to relieve herself.

Her blood hunger increased, too, and she began to hunt. She was much better at hunting than Reginald. Once, on an overnight trip to Paris, Nikki caught, fed on, and glamoured a young French woman while Reginald was waiting in line for a crepe at the foot of the Eiffel Tower. When she returned, she told him, "I'm so hungry after all that eating!" Then she ate three crepes, said how glad she was that she could no longer gain weight, and then picked Reginald up over her head and ran with him into a nearby cluster of hedges.

When the night came for Balestro's return, Reginald, Maurice, and Nikki took a train to Munich, rented a car, and drove south under Reginald's direction. After a half hour, they pulled into an empty parking lot at the foot of a massive hill with a feeling like doom. Karl and the other

EU Vampire Council members, who'd said they'd show up but would travel on foot, hadn't yet arrived.

"Has it occurred to anyone else," said Nikki, playing with the car's door handle without opening the door, "that what we're about to do really isn't much different from what those nutjobs do when they've predicted the end of the world? I mean, it must feel like this. At a certain time, head up to a certain place and wait for a certain hour, at which point some crazy thing is supposed to happen."

"Yes," said Reginald.

It hadn't just *occurred* to him; the idea had more or less *consumed* him. Over the past two weeks, with the deadline looming, he'd felt as if he were on a bizarre and foolish countdown to destiny. On one side of his mind, he remembered talking to Balestro and he remembered talking to the voice in the anteroom. When those things had happened, he had totally and completely believed in angels and armageddon, and it had all made sense. But now, when he thought about those things or the hill or the end of the vampire world, the other side of his mind dismissed it all and told him that he was a giant retard. That was the terminology it used, too.

"We were all there, and I totally believe in Reginald's location-scouting," said Maurice, leaning forward to stick his head between the front seats. "If Balestro doesn't show, it's because he's ditching us, not because it's not true."

"Maybe this is a cosmic joke," said Nikki. "Maybe we're on universal *Candid Camera*." She shivered in the chill night, not because she was cold, but because it fit the mood. "I just keep thinking that as sure as we are, so are those doomsayer cults. Where is our Kool Aid?"

They got out of the car and looked up at the top of the hill, at the huge rock at its top.

"That's a big hill," said Reginald.

"I'm going to head up," said Maurice. "Not trying to be rude. I just want to get the jump on things."

Reginald and Nikki nodded at him to go ahead, and in less than a second they saw Maurice appear far above, now very small, pacing around the rock.

"You can go up too," said Reginald. They'd begun to climb and he was already short on breath.

"Don't be a dickhead," she said, taking his hand.

The hill was steep. He fought to keep his breath.

"Want me to carry you?"

Reginald shook his head. "Leave me *some* dignity," he said.

A few minutes later, Nikki shook her head. "I wasn't kidding about what I said earlier," she said. "Part of me very seriously expects that we'll sit up here all night and nothing will happen, and then we'll go home in the morning feeling stupid, and life will go on."

"That would be okay with me," said Reginald.

"I believe in this — in all of it," she said. "But it's just so surreal. The world doesn't end every day. And look around us, Reginald." She made a sweeping motion with her arms, taking in the sprawling countryside. "The American Council and the American vampires you know didn't believe us. The Europeans believe us, but hell, who knows if they'll show? We're three people in the middle of nowhere in the middle of the night, climbing to a giant sacrificial altar... or something. How often have three people been right and tens of thousands been wrong?"

"History is created by crazy individuals who believed in something stupid and impossible," said Reginald.

"Why is it our job to save the world?" she said. "If we're right, we shouldn't have to do this alone."

"Karl and the others will show."

"Maybe."

"And we're not saving the world. I give us a ten percent chance of saving anything, including ourselves. Really, we're just choosing to be the first to die."

"Oh, well, that changes things," said Nikki. "Now I'm all for it."

It took them ten more minutes to reach the top of the hill. The rock, Reginald realized, did look like a giant sacrificial altar, which was unsettling. He mentioned it to Maurice, who knew the history of the area, and Maurice assured him that yes, sacrifices did happen here. It was, in a way, why they were there.

"I'll be the one to say it," said Nikki. "We're at a place of sacrifice, and we're not the high priests. Does that implication bother anyone?"

"I think it's pretty cool," said a voice.

Nikki turned as if her head were on a swivel. She found nothing, but then looked down and located the source of the voice and gave a moan. It was Claire.

"Claire?"

"And mom," said Claire, indicating a second, taller person now arriving at the top of the hill. "I can't drive. It would be absurd to think I'd just show up here by myself."

Reginald was enjoying the look on Nikki's face. He said, "There's a scene in one of the *Highlander* movies — the third one, I think — where someone inexplicably shows up thousands of miles away from home to find someone they know on a random mountaintop. And the first person says to the other, 'I knew I'd find you here.'"

"Right," said Claire. "I knew I'd find you here, Nikki. Reginald. Maurice."

Maurice looked much less surprised than Nikki. Nikki looked from one man to the other and stared into their impassive faces. Then she met the eyes of Claire's mother, Victoria. Victoria introduced herself to Nikki with a smile, as if they were meeting at a coffee shop for lunch.

"Why are you here, Claire?" said Nikki.

"Reginald called," she said.

"What a lovely rock," said Victoria, touching the stone.

Nikki shook her head, then turned to Reginald.

"Let's not play the game where I act all surprised and try to get the story out of you. How about you just tell me what happened here?" she said.

"I Skyped Claire. Asked her to put her mother on. Victoria thought it was very strange that her daughter was video chatting with the fat guy from her gymnastics class, but then she understood, and then I suggested they pack up their bags and take a European vacation. And here we are."

"When?" said Nikki.

"Last night."

"You can't glamour over video," said Maurice. "Vampire sociopaths have been trying to do it since the advent of television."

"Well," said Reginald, "in that case, I must just have made a really good case for dropping everything, running to the airport, and taking an international flight in order to meet strangers on top of a remote German hilltop at midnight."

Maurice's eyes rolled down, pensive.

"We saw *Dumb and Dumber* on the plane," said Claire. "It was terrible."

"It's dated," said Reginald.

"No," said Claire. "I can tell it was horrible when it was made."

"It's really cold up here all of a sudden," Victoria said vacantly.

Nikki was pacing. "Why, Reginald? You know why we're here. This isn't a tourist trip. We went to such great lengths last time to protect her, and this time she was half a world away and you brought her *into the danger zone.*"

"Thanks," said a new voice. "Now I'm going to have 'Highway to the Danger Zone' stuck in my head for a week." The three vampires turned to watch as Kenny Loggins crested the hill. Then Kenny added, "My songs are sticky. How do you think I won all those Grammys?"

Claire was nonplussed by Loggins's arrival. She meandered off to find her mother, who'd crossed to the other side of the massive rock so that she could read all of the inscriptions that had been carved into it over the years.

"Kenny," said Reginald.

"Reginald," said Kenny Loggins.

"Holy crap, it *is* cold," said Nikki.

"Oh, Jesus," said Maurice. Then, to Reginald: "Why is *he* here?"

And Reginald said, "Trust me."

A moment later, Reginald was pulling Nikki away from Kenny Loggins and explaining to Loggins that she was no longer human and therefore wouldn't interest him. Loggins seemed disappointed. Then Victoria and Claire rounded the rock and came back into view. When Kenny Loggins saw them, he was so shocked that he turned into Hervé Villechaize.

"Um," said Hervé Villechaize. He was so small that he could have hidden behind Reginald's legs, so he did until Reginald stepped away and kicked him, figuring he owed him one anyway for the treadmill prank last month.

"Hello," said Claire.

"Hello," said Victoria, bending forward at the waist to meet Villechaize eye-to-eye.

"Hey," said Villechaize, shaking her hand. "I've never met you before."

Nikki put a hand on Reginald's shoulder and turned him away from the group. Maurice would be able to hear what she said, of course, but the woman, the girl, and Villechaize wouldn't.

"Help me out here," she said.

"Look," said Reginald. "They'll be safe. They're on the winning side, remember?"

"But *whyyyy*," Nikki whined. This had to be exhausting for her. Not physically, but mentally. Reginald himself, on the other hand, finally felt like he was hitting his stride.

"The angels want evolution, right? Well, I've formed a friendly relationship with someone I was supposed to feed on. And in turn, she kept me alive."

"You can hardly be the first vampire who's done that," she said.

Reginald shrugged. "Claire can be quite persuasive," he said. "Besides, we have nothing else. No harm, no foul. I even paid for their flight and hotel using Walker's credit card."

Nikki eyed him. It was most definitely an eyeing, seeming to bore into him and ask if he was really telling her the truth.

"And Kenny Loggins?" She looked over, then looked back after realizing that Loggins had made a change. "I mean, the midget?" she amended, giving no indication that she found Kenny Loggins, Hervé Villechaize, or one becoming the other at all odd.

"That's Altus. He's an incubus. Shape shifter and seducer of women. I'd keep your distance. You'll be immune as a vampire, but he's still an asshole."

"Incubus? I thought they were women."

"That's a succubus. Incubi are male. They screw

women in the night. You should read the accounts. The way it's written, it's like a surprise, like these women turn around and suddenly realize they'd been screwed by a demon, and are all like, 'Dammit, not again!'"

"They're like a shape-shifting Todd Walker," said Nikki.

"Exactly."

"So why is he here?"

Reginald shrugged. "Comic relief?"

Behind them, Victoria was telling Hervé Villechaize, "I loved you in *Fantasy Island.*" Villechaize was trying to slink away, to hide behind Maurice. Maurice didn't owe him for a treadmill prank, but he kicked him repeatedly anyway. Again and again. And again. The woman and girl either didn't notice the overt violence or didn't care.

Suddenly, the entire hilltop seemed to come alive. The rock shook, and Hervé Villechaize fell to the ground, the impact jarring him into what seemed to be Altus's default shape of a good-looking tall man with shoulder-length dark blonde hair.

Smoke and fire belched from nowhere, and a shape began to resolve in front of them. Victoria watched the giant rock altar with a wide grin plastered on her face as if she were watching a stage show. Claire looked enraptured, as if she'd never seen anything so engaging. Reginald thought dimly that her awe had to be magnified if the last thing she'd seen was *Dumb and Dumber*.

When the fire was gone and the smoke had dwindled to a few remaining wisps curling into the night sky, the imposing figure of Balestro in his familiar scary old man shape stood in front of them. He looked the same as the last time Reginald had seen him — white-haired, with very severe eyes. He trained the eyes on each one of them in turn.

"I come today as a representative of the founding Six, who fell from grace, who created Cain and Abel, who set the game in motion aeons past, who…"

"Yeah, we got this already," said Reginald.

Balestro stopped, then re-gathered himself. "Your time has expired. You understand?"

"I understand."

"And you lay down willingly?"

"Not at all. I offer myself as an agent of evolution for the vampire species. You're all omniscient and stuff. You can see what's in my mind?"

"Of course," said Balestro.

"So… then you know how awesome it is. Check it out. Pretty good, right?"

"I guess."

Maurice whispered in his ear, asking just what the hell he was doing.

"Showing off," said Reginald. Then to the angel, he said, "Check this out."

He reached down, placed one oddly-shaped rock at his foot, precariously balanced a second rock on top of the first, then found a third rock and balanced it on top. The rickety tower of three looked ready to fall when Reginald grabbed the top rock and kicked his legs up so that he was doing a one-handed handstand on top of the rocks, all of which had become perfectly still and balanced.

"Neat trick," said the angel, unamused.

"That's nothing," said Reginald. "Give me two numbers." He was still upside down, but now he was scissoring his legs as if doing an upside-down jig. A coin had appeared in his free hand. He held the hand out to the side and made the coin jump across his knuckles. Then the coin hopped into the air and landed back on his hand. He said, without looking at the coin, "Heads."

Then he flipped the coin again. "Heads." Again. "Tails."

"That's amazing," said Altus. Then, to the angel, he said, "He's getting these right. It's aweso..."

"Enough!" said the angel.

"Heads. Tails. Tails."

"And you are?" said Victoria, extending a hand to the angel on the altar.

Nikki tugged at Reginald's pantleg, which was falling down, exposing his long black socks and hairy calves. "Get *down!* He's just getting pissed off."

"Oh *no*," said Reginald. "I've pissed off someone who's going to kill us all no matter what we do?"

"Stop it!"

Maurice was pacing, taking in the scene: fiery Balestro, upside-down Reginald, protesting Nikki, perplexed Altus, polite Victoria, and interested Claire. He put his hand to his chin, thinking.

"Hey Maurice," said Reginald. "Tell Mr. Balestro about how you drove off four fellow vampires and then turned me to save me, out of compassion for someone who was supposed to be prey. Tell him about how I saved Claire here."

Claire scoffed. "You didn't save me."

"How I've resisted biting Claire today, despite all the chances she's given me," Reginald clarified.

"Yeah," Claire said to the angel, seeming to realize that impressing the man on the altar was important.

"And he's a good gymnast," Victoria added helpfully.

"Tell me," Reginald said to the angel, hopping off of his rock tower and back onto his feet. "What would you have wanted of us?"

"We have given you your answers already," said Balestro.

"I see. So… development. Evolution. Not just numbers, but the ability to adapt, change and grow. Right?"

Balestro looked uncertain for a moment. "Yes. But it is too late. You have stagnated. You are a failed experiment."

"That's so hurtful," said Reginald. He pouted. "Look around. We're *quite* evolved. All three of us. Hell, Nikki opted to become one of us just two weeks before you were due to kill us all. If that's not a statement of belief in the future of the species, I don't know what is."

"You're three," said Balestro, "out of seventy thousand."

"*Fourteen thousand* and three," said a voice behind them. It was Karl, and with him were the twelve members of the European Vampire Council. Karl's hair was done up high and extravagant, dyed white, surely a conscious homage to Gary Oldman's portrayal of Count Dracula.

Balestro looked furious.

"Technically thirteen only today," Karl said, "but we number over fourteen thousand in the EU. We speak for them. East will come along. So maybe you kill just the American vampires. They started *Twilight*."

"*Karl!*" Maurice hissed.

"Okay, fine," he said. "You kill nobody."

Reginald saw Balestro's eyes flash red. The old body in front of them was just a skin, and behind it was the power of Heaven, or Hell, or both. Reginald felt sure that if any of them were to attack the body, Balestro could become a pillar of fire able to lay waste to the Earth.

"Promising change does not change the game," said Balestro. "Promising change does not guarantee change. It does not alter the losing position of your pieces."

Karl wrapped his arms around his torso and said, "Why is it so damned cold up here?"

"You gave us thirty days," said Reginald. "That's not enough time. It's only enough time to decide. To persuade. And we're persuaded and can persuade more. Now we know what you want and you've shown what you can do. Let us, *en masse*, convince the rest. Give us time to do what you want of us."

"It's too late."

"You choose to forfeit? You choose to willingly give up, now, when you have the promise of fourteen thousand people?"

"*Promises*," said Balestro. He said it like it was an obscenity.

"And you're just one. We've given you new information. There are six of you. You can make this decision by yourself, isolated in human form?"

"Go ahead," said Karl. "Take a thousand years to decide. And if you have to kill the American vampires, is okay."

"*Karl!*" Maurice hissed.

Karl shrugged. "I'm just saying, I'm okay for compromise if needed."

Balestro appeared indecisive. It was Reginald's mention of the other angels that had done it. According to lore, the Six always made decisions in joint, and Reginald and Karl had added to the equation. He'd no longer be carrying out a decided-upon directive if he laid waste to the vampires of the world without returning to the anteroom first. He'd be making a unilateral decision to ignore new information.

"No," said Balestro. "We are no longer willing to support you, and you are unworthy to represent us."

He raised his hands. Reginald could feel a charge run through the air. The hair on the back of his neck, on his arms, even on his head began to stand up. He looked to Nikki and Maurice. They'd felt it too.

A breeze began to stir, and a fire began to swirl on the horizon to the east. Then to the north. Then to the west. And then they watched as they were surrounded by a ring of fire. But it wasn't fire at all. It was some kind of energy. Altus, Claire, and Victoria couldn't see it. Reginald could tell that much by looking at them. The fire was only for vampire eyes. He wondered if every vampire in the world was seeing it. He wondered if every vampire in the world could, right now, hear the angel's voice in their heads, as he could, as Balestro began counting down in their minds.

Ten. Nine.

"Okay," said Reginald. "Then I'd like to introduce you to Claire." And Reginald put a hand on Claire's shoulder.

Balestro kept his hands high. The fire grew. The voice became louder: *Seven. Six.*

"And her mother," said Reginald, extending a hand, palm up, toward Victoria.

Four.

"And her father, of course."

Three.

Balestro lowered his hands. The fire receded a bit, waiting. The countdown stopped.

Reginald's other hand had extended in the other direction, now pointing at Altus the incubus.

The countdown stopped. The fire waited, now changing from a fiery red to a quiescent blue. Reginald could almost feel all of the world's vampires waiting, watching.

"It is true," said Balestro.

Behind them, Karl barked laughter.

"What?" said Claire.

"Claire," said Victoria suddenly. "Why aren't you wearing a coat?"

Reginald went down on one knee and turned Claire around, both of his hands on her shoulders.

"Claire," he said. "Six months ago, I spent an hour in the middle of every night in your living room, watching TV while your mother slept upstairs. Not once did she wake up. Not once did she come down. Not once did she stir. Didn't that strike you as strange?"

"She was drunk," said Claire.

"No. She was under the influence, but not of alcohol. Not all of the time, anyway." He looked up at Altus. Claire's gaze followed his, and Altus turned around, suddenly very interested in the stone altar.

"She didn't recently get clean," he said. "She recently *became free*. When she lost her job, the thing that has had a hold over her for your entire life stopped seeing her walk by the place where it lives, and it lost interest, and it moved to someone else, and it let her go. It wasn't her fault, Claire."

He let go of her shoulders and she turned, taking her glamoured mother by the hand.

Balestro looked down at Claire. He said, "Speak."

"Um... what?"

Nikki's lips were at Reginald's ear. "What just happened?"

Maurice was looking at Reginald with curiosity, as were several members of the EU Council. So, loud enough for everyone to hear, Reginald told Nikki, "Usually, incubi just toy with women, getting their rocks off. They seldom get women pregnant, and when they do, the children never make it to full term. So far, so good, Altus?"

Altus nodded self-consciously.

"Except for one time," said Karl, moving up to stand next to Reginald. "*Only* one time, an incubus had a child of a woman. The child's name was Merlin."

"What?" said Claire.

"Speak," repeated Balestro, looking down.

"What does he want me to do?" Claire whispered to Reginald.

"He wants you to do the one thing he can't," said Reginald. "He wants you to tell the future."

FIFTEEN

Prescient

The blue ring of fire continued to circle, continued to churn. Claire looked up at Reginald, then at the angel. Reginald gave her a small nod.

"Uh…" said Claire.

"If you have nothing to say," said Balestro, "we'll continue."

"Uh…" said Claire. She tugged on her mother's pant-leg. Victoria looked down, a wide smile on her face. Finding no help there, Claire looked back at Reginald.

"Fine," said Balestro. He raised his hands again. The fire swelled.

"Wait!" said Claire.

Balestro lowered his hands. The fire shrunk again, became blue again.

"It's like Reginald said. They're going to evolve. He'll… uh… he'll show them the way."

"What way?"

"The smart way." She waved her hands around in mystical-looking spirals. "It is thus predicted. *Shazam.*"

Balestro looked up at Reginald. Squinted. Then he looked back at Claire.

"Tell me more," he said.

"There's… uh… a great change coming. A war, between humans and vampires." She looked up, having caught Reginald making sharp head-shaking motions and drawing a finger across his throat. "Wait. Not really a war," she continued. "Like a skirmish. Yes. I see it now in the third eye. It'll be all good. And then there will be change. Like, you know, good change."

"A war?" said Balestro.

"Just a little one. Nothing to get worked up about. I mean, just a few skirmishes to, like, clear out the pipes, you know? Shake things up. There will be… uh… bad vampires. And… like, some good ones. But…" Her eyes jumped open as if something brilliant had just occurred to her. "Oh! Like, lots of *evolved* ones, like, you know, *evolved* vampires. Like Reginald! And they'll use their big brains and become more. Uh… Like, they'll invent stuff like that True Blood blood substitute or whatever, which isn't to say that they'll be, like, sellouts, you understand… but, like, that makes them more flexible." She looked at the angel, met his icy glare. "But they'll still be evil! Not too evil. Like, the perfect amount of evil. Like, what I'm saying is, here: They'll be the hunters they're supposed to be, and they'll drink blood and be eternal and all, but they won't be assholes. Oh, sorry, Mom. They won't be jerks, I mean. They'll… what?"

She turned her head to look at Reginald, who was doing an odd dance with his chin held high and his lips pursed, his expression superior, his hands tugging at imaginary tuxedo lapels. Then he made big X motions over himself. He stopped when Balestro looked over.

"And the vampires will… not be fancy? They won't

be… uh… gay? No! No, I guess they'll be gay sometimes." Her eyes were darting back and forth between Reginald and Balestro, trying to read a frantic game of charades.

"Pompous!" she yelled, suddenly triumphant. "Yeah, that's what it was… uh… I mean, what 'the eye' was trying to tell me. All the stuff they do now, with, like, trying to be some sort of a super race, that's over. Like, in the near future."

Balestro thought for a second. Then he said, "Why?"

"Why what?"

"Your… *vision*… says that vampires are going to stop pursuing a bottleneck of perfection. If this is true, why would it be?"

"I don't know," said Claire, offended. "I don't write the songs. I just play them."

"I'm sure it's because they recognize that evolution doesn't come from the bottleneck you mention," said Reginald. He dropped his eyes to the ground when Balestro snapped his head over to look at him.

"Yeah," said Claire. "I see Reginald leading a lot of this stuff, so there you go." She made jazz hands. "Booga-booga."

Balestro stood tall on the altar. The blue fire continued to roil. Reginald watched it, seeing it boil past trees and rocks and leaving them untouched. It was in his mind. It was in all of their minds. What would happen if Balestro unleashed it? Would vampires simply explode? Or would they have the vampire equivalents of embolisms, quietly breaking inside and falling apart? He could feel Maurice's consciousness inside of his mind — and now, joining it, Nikki's as well. Through Maurice, he could sense dozens of others, and through them, scores of others. A giant family tree stretched below him in the recesses of his mind, and he was sure — yes, *sure* now — that every vampire alive was watching the ring of fire wherever they were, knowing exactly what it was, waiting to see what would happen.

"I can't read her," said Balestro, looking down at Claire.

"Strange," said Reginald. "I can."

"I couldn't read Merlin either," said Balestro. Then he looked at Reginald. "But *you*, I can read." He looked at Maurice. "And you. And the rest of you." He sighed. Reginald wondered if sighing was a human affect, something he did because it was a habit of the flesh. Did angels sigh in Heaven?

The fire blinked out like an exhausted gas flame and was gone.

"You, I can read," Balestro repeated. And then, without warning, something came out of Balestro and blew through Reginald like a shotgun blast. He felt his head come off, watched as his vision went a brilliant white and then black. The world spun and he hit the ground, his head an arm's length away, and he could see it now, and he reached out his hand for it and his neck was ragged and bleeding and he could feel his pulse, could feel his life leaving him, and then...

And then he was standing where he'd been a moment earlier, intact, and nothing had happened after all.

But something *had* happened. But something had changed.

"We will be watching," said Balestro.

And then, accompanied by the fire and light show that had heralded his arrival, he was gone.

SIXTEEN

28 Days Later

"You are the biggest nerd ever," said Nikki. "You've got carte blanche to do whatever you want with a hot girl, and this is how you spend it."

"Shut up," said Reginald. His fingers touched ceramic, backed off, touched it again.

Nikki grabbed the front of her shirt and jiggled her breasts dramatically.

"Stop it. I'm trying to think," he said.

"See? Right there. The fact that you care about the game at all proves your nerdness. I'll bet I could get action if I had giant cinnamon buns on the side of my head like Princess Leia. Let's lay down on this board and get nasty."

"There's a war on," said Reginald. "Is that all you can think of?"

"There's not a war on," said Nikki.

"Give it time."

Reginald's intuition on the hilltop had proven correct. Whatever Balestro had done with the ring of fire was evidence of Balestro's — and, presumably, the others' — dominion over their creations. Every vampire he'd encountered in the days following the hilltop events had seen the blue ring of flame. Every one knew exactly what it had been: *Extinction.* There was nothing they could have done about it. The phenomenon was psychic, inside of their collective minds. There was no way to fight something that came from within. They were only alive because Balestro had let them live. Because he had chosen, not because of anything else.

"She was just making it up," said Nikki. "It's a talent that girls around you seem to be required to learn."

"She thought she was," said Reginald. "But I doubt she *actually* was. She has power she doesn't recognize yet. I wasn't making it up about Altus and Claire. Balestro would have known if I was. The second master wizard ever and I'm already in good with her. What are the chances?"

"Exactly. What *are* the chances?"

Reginald sat up from his semi-reclined position and ate one of the cheese nachos on the plate at his side. "Impossible chances. It could really only have happened by plan."

"How?"

"What am I, an angel?"

Nikki leaned forward and kissed him. "I'm not rising to that rather obvious dig for a compliment," she said. "But nice try."

Reginald made his move. Rather quickly, Nikki made her answering move, and then started tapping her fingers on the table, indicating that Reginald should hurry up yet again.

"Don't rush me."

"Come on, smarty pants," she said.

He moved his lips against each other, thoughtfully.

Then she said, "You really think there's a war coming?"

"There's *something* coming. You've seen the Council.

Bunch of idiots. It's like they were given a choice between right or left and were told that left led off a cliff. And so they chose to go up."

"I don't understand that metaphor. As usual."

"Exactly. It doesn't make sense."

Nikki waited for elaboration. None came.

"Charles, with his little crusade. You think he's trouble?"

Reginald scoffed. "Come on! You're prescient enough to know the answer to that. Charles, like so many of our other friends, has taken the simplest set of directions in the world and read them incorrectly."

"Ah," said Nikki. "That's him 'going up' instead of going right or even left, in your metaphor."

"Correct."

"Because he's going the wrong way. Because he read the directions wrong."

"Exactly."

"It's as if you had a wagon full of hay, and suddenly Al Roker showed up," said Nikki. "That's a perfect metaphor for the situation."

Reginald ignored her.

"Are you ever going to move?" she said.

Reginald placed his hand on his remaining rook and moved it across the board, to check Nikki's king.

"Check."

Nikki moved. Reginald countered.

"Check," he said again.

Nikki threw her hands up and hooted. Then she moved her queen in front of her king, checkmating Reginald's king.

"Nikki one, Reginald one hundred!" she hooted. "I'm hot on your tail, baby!"

Reginald smirked, tipped his king, and sat up. "Well done, Nik."

"You owe me first bite."

Reginald tipped his head to the side, exposing his neck as a tease, then cocked it back to neutral and smiled.

Nikki batted her eyelashes. "Should I put cinnamon buns on the sides of my head?"

"That would be so hot," he said, smiling. Then the smile melted away. "Seriously. Do you have any cinnamon buns? Don't put them on your hair, though. That would be gross. On a plate is fine."

"I don't want a cinnamon bun. I've lost my taste for everything but coffee. I want your blood, and then I want to go out and feed for real. I'll catch you a nice young man."

"The buns are both for me," said Reginald. Then, because it was an obvious move, he reached out and grabbed *her* buns as she stood from her chair. Then he got up, and he followed her.

Inside of Reginald's head, Balestro's gift pulsed like a second heart.

The Story Continues

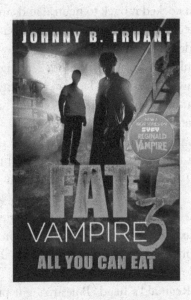

Angels and Demons, Myths and Legends…

This sequel to the cult hit picks up where Fat Vampire left off, following a trio of unlikely heroes down a path of myth and superstition into truths that have been buried for centuries.

Keep on reading Johnny B. Truant's blockbuster series, and you'll never look at vampires (or vampire stories) the same way again.

A Note from the Author

Thanks for reading *Fat Vampire 2: Tastes Like Chicken.*

If you liked it please leave a review on your favorite bookselling site so others can enjoy it too. A couple of sentences would mean a lot to me.

Thank you!

Johnny B Truant

Also by Johnny B. Truant

The Fat Vampire Series

Fat Vampire

Fat Vampire 2: Tastes Like Chicken

Fat Vampire 3: All You Can Eat

Fat Vampire 4: Harder, Better, Fatter, Stronger

Fat Vampire 5: Fatpocaplypse

Fat Vampire 6: Survival of the Fattest

The Fat Vampire Chronicles

The Vampire Maurice

Anarchy and Blood

Vampires in the White City

Fangs and Fame

About the Author

Johnny B. Truant is co-owner of the Sterling & Stone Story Studio, an IP powerhouse focusing on books and adaptations for film and television. It's the best job in the world, and he spends his days creating cool stuff with partners Sean Platt and David W. Wright, as well as more than 20 gifted storytellers.

Johnny is the bestselling author of over 100 books under various pen names, including the Fat Vampire and Invasion series. On the nonfiction side, he's also co-author of the indie publishing mainstay Write. Publish. Repeat. and co-host of the weekly Story Studio Podcast.

Originally from Ohio, Johnny and his family now live in Austin, Texas, where he's finally surrounded by creative types as weird as he is.

9 781629 551326